LAINEE DELANEY: STICKS IN STONE

Lainee Delaney Series, Vol. 3

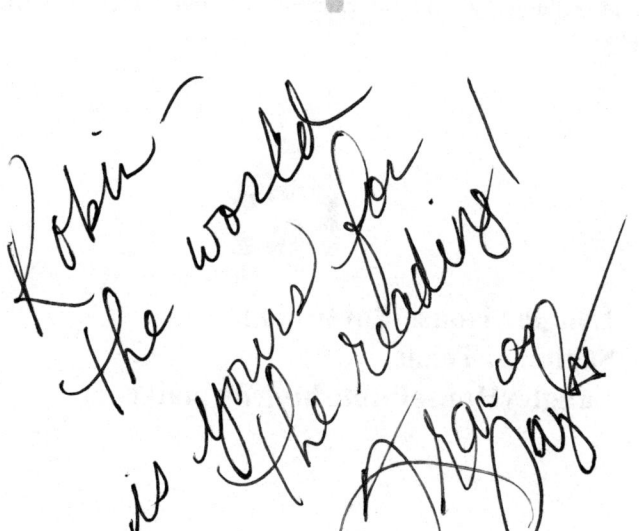

BY FRANCES LANGLEY

Copyright 2017 Frances Langley
All Rights Reserved
Print Edition, July 2018

Publisher's Note: This is a work of fiction. All characters and events portrayed in this book are fictional, and any resemblance to real people or incidents is purely coincidental.

All rights reserved. No part of the book may be reproduced in any form or by any means without the prior written consent of the Author or Publisher, with the exception of brief quotes to be used in reviews.

Langley House Publishing
Saginaw, Texas
LangleyHousePublishing@gmail.com

ISBN-10:   0-9988311-4-X
ISBN-13:   978-0-9988311-4-5

THE REVIEWS ARE IN

"*Sticks in Stone*, the third installment in the Lainee Delaney series was worth the wait! I have followed this series and each book has drawn me further in the world of my favorite Southern belle and private investigator. This book showed the growth of the character and the depth of Lainee, even more so than its predecessors. I enjoyed not only her charm, but also loved seeing the darker side of Lainee; the side which reflected her incredible skill as a detective and her survival skill with her protective nature. I also have a major book crush on Sticks, so it was AWESOME to have him get so much page time! He is sexy and "gets Lainee" like no other.

I believe the talented author Frances Langley has developed a character that will be around a long time! I look forward to the future adventures of the sweet and sassy Ms. Delaney and encourage this read for all who loves mysteries, private detective novels, or women's fiction! A Must Read!"

Michelle Cornwell Jordan, 4CWMedia Productions

PRAISE FOR THE SERIES

"Humorous and a page turner to see what happens next!! Definitely hope this private investigator has more adventures for us readers!"

Marilyn Simmons

"A fun page-turner! Lainee is a cute character with a lot of spunk who gets herself into some interesting situations. I enjoyed her first adventure and look forward to the next one!"

Tiffany Wood

Chapter One
The Death Plane

My third flight. Ever. And I was going to die.

The turbulence had come out of nowhere over New Mexico on my flight from Arizona back to Texas. A teen-aged girl in the seat across the aisle muffled a scream as a few children throughout the plane were beginning to cry.

Touching the rosary worn around my neck, I said a quick prayer to Saint Christopher for safe travels. Thankfully, my last few days were spent taking Catechism classes to appease my new husband's mother. Correction: after the scene I just left, my soon-to-be ex-husband.

I discovered I was as good of a Catholic as I had been a Baptist because I began to question whether Christopher was the patron saint for travelers. I altered the prayer to include Saints Francis and Jude. For added good measure, I threw in Saints Peter, Paul, Nicholas, Patrick, and Valentine, along with Mother Mary.

My thoughts went to my poor husband. I should have waited to fly with him but leaving seemed the easier way out. Of course, I hadn't considered having to haul my own luggage everywhere at the time.

The plane jolted once more, and I took the head-between-the-knees position, cursing the circumstances that brought me to this situation. Had it been only four days ago? It had all started with my first words as a married woman. "Torres. So, you're Hispanic? I thought you were Asian."

Leave it to Lainee Delaney to marry a man when she didn't even know his name, but that's how most events happened in my life lately. Long-term goals and I had recently parted ways. My life was lived one moment at a time. I never knew what would transpire next, which was probably why I had such high anxiety. I hated surprises.

In response to my question, Clint, a.k.a. Sticks, a.k.a. hot FBI agent and medical doctor, had kissed my forehead.

"There's so much for you to learn. This is going to be fun."

***

It all started when my Southern belle logic made me assume meeting Sticks's parents was the appropriate thing to do.

We had entered through the side door leading to the kitchen of the small wood-framed house. "Yo, ma," Sticks scanned the room. Food was warming on the stove and in the oven. A smorgasbord lined the counters and spread onto the dining table. His parents were prepared to feed a multitude, but no one appeared to be home.

"She might answer you if you didn't say, "Yo, Ma.' That's not the politest way to address your mother."

"I'm saying Eomma," it sounded more like 'ee yoh ma' when he said it slowly. "E-O-M-M-A. It's Korean for mom, Miss Manners." He tapped my nose playfully and we chuckled at the memory of his pet name for me.

"Eomma," he repeated louder, as he reached for my hand. "I have some amazing news for you." Still holding onto me, he led the way through the shuttered swinging doors into the living room.

"Surprise!" About fifteen people yelled as we entered. Everyone was standing. The room was too cramped for anyone to have hidden.

Sticks let go of me as the group approached to hug him or shake his hand. He introduced me simply as Lainee to all of his cousins, aunts, and uncles who were gathered.

One small Asian woman stood alone in the corner, anger in her eyes as she watched the scene. Minute in stature, yet still commanding, everyone gave her a wide berth. When the activity began to die down, she approached. The woman grabbed my left hand and looked at the ring, then glanced at Sticks's ring and said in patchy English, "Thi' amazing new you need tell me?" She began crying.

Sticks stepped toward his mom to give her a comforting hug. Instead, she slapped the side of his head. "Why you not let us know? Ween you get marry? Why we not invi'ed?"

The group laughed as they collectively took two steps back, not wanting to be too close to his mother's wrath. An older Hispanic male found the courage to separate himself from the crowd and put his arm around Sticks's mom. "Come on now, Kimmie. You know Clint does things his own way."

After the extended family left, Sticks and I moved our things to his childhood bedroom—not the most romantic venue for a wedding night. I hung up my clothing items and put more in one of his lesser-filled dresser drawers, leaving the intimate apparel and accessories in one of my smaller garment bags. I was certain his mother had not changed anything since he had left. There were remnants of game pieces, smoothed stones, and old ticket stubs in the drawer.

His walls were covered with ribbons and certificates of achievement and had shelves of trophies. There were also various types of sporting equipment neatly arranged on hooks throughout the room. He was the All-American boy, who just happened to be the son of an Asian immigrant mother and the grandson of Mexican immigrant grandparents.

From the dates on the trophies, I did some quick calculations and determined he was around thirty-two. That meant my new husband was about eight years older than me. These kinds of things were good to know. Granted, it was even better if one knew them before the marriage.

I was looking at photos pinned on a bulletin board as Sticks came up behind me, wrapped his arms around my waist, and nuzzled my neck. "Sorry you were ambushed by the whole family. I would have much preferred to introduce you as Mrs. Torres in a more private setting."

"Mrs. Delaney-Torres," I corrected.

"Well, let's leave that out of the conversation with my mom for a while." He began kissing my neck and I turned to respond more appropriately. The action was halted by a knock on the door.

"Clint?" his mother yelled in her strong Korean accent. She had made the English language her own hodgepodge of words without ending sounds, prepositions, or helping verbs. "Dad and I wan' talk you and wife."

Sticks let out a frustrated moan, which was much different from the one he had done merely seconds before the knock when my hand had gotten somewhat adventurous. "You're going to have to go out there first. I need to wait a few minutes before I'll be able to make it."

Chapter Two
The Interrogation Begins

I checked my appearance in the mirror and tucked a few stray hairs behind my ears. Sticks gave me a sympathetic look as I walked to the door, opening it slightly and squeezing through so his mom would have a limited view of him in his predicament.

"Sticks is still unpacking. He'll be out when he's finished."

"Sticks? Why you call him that? His name Clint." The minimal friendliness she had shown me when Sticks, I meant Clint, was present disappeared. She walked down the short hallway then turned sharply and said, "Come, now."

I followed her to the living room where Mr. Torres was lounging in his recliner. I got the feeling if they had been alone, he would have been sleeping with one hand tucked in his waistband.

"You not answer question," Mrs. Torres accused.

That was because it was not so easy to answer. I wasn't sure what Clint's parents knew about his job. I wasn't even sure I knew all his job entailed. Would they be shocked to know he was rappelling out of helicopters, tracking mafia leaders, or performing medical procedures with do-it-yourself equipment?

I decided to go with only the basic facts. "I got injured while hiking with friends. It seemed minor to me, but when Sticks found us, he noticed my wound was infected. He crafted a makeshift stretcher by putting sticks and a tarp together. I didn't know his name, so I called him Sticks, and it just kind of … stuck."

Those statements summarized the facts I was kidnapped and escaped, all while trying to rescue Dylan, someone I had briefly dated. During the same ordeal, Dylan's older brother Cade, who was another ex-boyfriend, along with one of my captors were shot. It was then that Sticks and his team of specially trained agents rescued us from the wilderness.

"That not goo' enough reason call him Sticks. We name him Clint. That name you use."

I let my manners slip a bit when I asked, "Well, why did you name him Clint?"

Mr. Torres reached over and touched Mrs. Torres's forearm, giving it a gentle pat, as he answered my question. "Kimmie grew up on outdated American culture. Her favorite show was *Rawhide* and her first love was for Clint Eastwood. I think she agreed to marry me so she would have a better chance to meet him. She's hung in here for thirty-five years, though. I might have a chance against him now."

As reasons for a name go, that was a pretty good one, so I decided to concede and call him Clint more often. At least in front of his mother. Mr. Torres was behaving much more cordially than Mrs. Torres. So, I decided to talk to him instead, hoping my new mother-in-law would calm down in the process. "It's impressive you have shown such a commitment to each other. Not many people accomplish that nowadays. How did you meet?"

His mother's lips tightened. It was clear she wasn't going to answer, so Mr. Torres said, "I joined the Army when I was eighteen and was stationed in South Korea. Kimmie and her mom sold vegetables in the market every week. I made sure I got my leave every Wednesday so I could be there. I don't think I've ever eaten so healthy in my life." He rubbed his bulging belly, emphasizing that was no longer the case. "I finally got the nerve to ask her to dinner. Her mother nearly scared me off when she came at me with a knife, but I remained patient and content with seeing her at the stand."

Mrs. Torres softened, somewhat, as she listened to her husband. That all changed when she turned toward me again. "What you do for living?"

What should I say? I had two options: One, I owned a private investigating business that operated in the red every month, or two, I substitute taught to supplement my trust fund allowance, which was spent mostly on the upkeep of, and taxes for, the estate my parents willed to me, in addition to paying the salaries of the household staff. To most people, I either sounded unsuccessful or spoiled. I doubted she would fall into the category of the few people who thought I was determined, so I kept it short and sweet. "I'm an educator and a detective."

"You both? You can't make decision?" She

crossed her arms over her chest. I wanted to point out that her precious Clint, being both a doctor and agent for the FBI, also had difficulty choosing a single career but refrained from making the comment. I wasn't going to disparage my husband in order to prove a point to his mother. After an awkward silence, she continued her interrogation. "Where you from?"

"I'm from a small town in Texas called Waco."

"Where fire burn?" She faced her husband. "She live with religious freaks. No good for Clint."

I sat on the edge of the couch. "That's not accurate. Everyone from Waco isn't a Branch Davidian. For example, I'm a Baptist and…"

His mother gasped. "Oh, that worse, Alejandro. She Protestant."

I could see Sticks coming down the hall and was hopeful he could provide a buffer.

"Clint, we talk to Lainee. Now tell us abou' wedding." She spoke with a gooey sweet tone as she got up to meet him and put her arm through his to walk the rest of the way to the couch, making sure she sat between us.

I thought I could rectify the situation. "It was a lovely ceremony. Simple, yet elegant." I pulled out my cell phone and showed her the few pictures Hilda, my housekeeper, had taken. She and her twin sister, Helga, were our witnesses. "I love the dress. Look at the intricate lace bodice and how the beaded belt draws your eye and emphasizes the contrast of the chiffon skirt."

Clint and I were the perfect couple in the photo.

Even with my three-inch heels, he stood about four inches taller than my five-foot-three frame. His broad shoulders and muscular build made me look delicate in his embrace. I was in profile gazing into his dark brown eyes that crinkled as he smiled down at me. I wore my long, dark, usually straight brown hair in a front updo with cascading, loose curls flowing down my back. My paler skin thankfully had enough sun exposure to appear tanned as my freckles had played connect the dots. The pose showcased my one-and-a-half carat asscher cut diamond ring, and with his arm wrapped around my waist, you could also see his simple gold band. Our hands were clasped at my side, fingers intertwined. Seeing the photo made me realize the gravity of my impulsive decision. I was now a married woman.

My stomach was in knots as I quickly swiped to the next photo and continued, "The peach hues add depth to my skin tone. It was perfect for the occasion, even though it was the dress I wore when I was maid of honor at my friend's wedding." Surely this gave her the impression I was resourceful and practical.

"Dress need more lace. Show too much. Probably why you not wear white. Why you not think my Clint worth new dress?"

Sticks defended me. "We planned the wedding in one day, Eomma. Lainee was amazing at getting all the details taken care of."

I was not going to give up on winning his mother over. "Yes, it all came together nicely. The florist was able to make the bouquet in less than an hour and the

Justice of the Peace was a friend of my dad's and..."

His mother stood. Her five-foot stature barely surpassed the height of the lounging Clint. "You not marry in church?"

When his mother began ranting in Korean, Sticks leaned forward with his elbows on his knees. He tucked his forehead in one hand and blew out a long breath.

Mr. Torres simply pushed the footrest down, making the recliner sit upright. "I'll go get the rollaway set up for Clint in your craft room, Kimmie."

Chapter Three
The Brace Position

My thoughts were jarred back to the flight, literally, when my cheek hit the leg of the man seated beside me. The plane tilted toward the right and began a rapid descent. With my head still tucked, I tightened my grip on my knees and let out an, "Oh, my lord."

"First flight?" a rich, baritone voice asked.

I turned my head so my words wouldn't be muffled. I wasn't going to waste any of my last moments on earth, or in this case, plummeting toward the earth, repeating small talk. "No, my third. Why do people keep asking me that?"

The captain's voice sounded overhead. "Ladies and gentlemen, we are being rerouted to El Paso International Airport due to severe weather over Texas. Please be sure to get a voucher from a flight attendant before leaving the plane to enjoy amenities offered by the airport shops and restaurants."

My seatmate waited for a flight attendant to complete her announcement of connecting flight options before answering my question. "Maybe because you're the only one in the brace position." He shifted in his seat and his tablet fell. He bent over to retrieve it, making me feel even more claustrophobic.

"By the way, you may want to rethink your safety plan. There're two popular theories about bracing in an airplane. One is that it doesn't help save lives and its purpose is actually to preserve teeth to make identifying bodies easier. The second is that it increases the chance of death, saving airlines and insurance companies millions in settlement costs from permanent injury claims."

I bolted upright thankful to, yet somewhat irritated at, the man who reminded me of the know-it-all Cade. I murmured a quiet, "Thank you."

"You shouldn't worry so much. No one else seems too concerned."

"What about that girl across the aisle? She's crying."

"Listen carefully. Her boyfriend texted her before the flight and broke up. She's being dramatic."

"What about the children? I can hear them crying, too."

"Children always cry on planes." The plane bumped again. He changed the subject, probably to offset my impending panic attack. "So, where'd you go on your other flights?"

"My first flight was after a tribute for my grandmother. She was from Georgia and fancied herself a Southern belle."

"Doesn't that make you one, too?"

"I say I am, but my friend tells me that's an insult considering I'm from Texas. She thinks Texans should have more pride than to be associated with Georgians and South Carolinians."

He chuckled. "Well, that attitude is another reason to avoid the Lone Star State."

I ignored his unintentional goading and continued my story. "Anyway, Grandma Elaine had wanted her ashes spread along the Mason-Dixon Line, but that was a difficult task to honor since she hadn't been cremated. Instead, after her burial in the family plot, my parents, siblings, their kids, and I rented an RV and drove along what we thought was the line. Then we realized we were really traveling the path of Sherman's March to the Sea. Despite Daddy being terrified of airplanes, he was so mad at my brother for planning the wrong trip, we wound up flying home."

"And the second?"

"Well, that was to meet my husband's parents."

"And you're taking your third flight alone, so I'm assuming it didn't go too well."

"No, it didn't." Thankfully, I didn't have to elaborate because the plane touched the ground, smoothly. The man had done a wonderful job of diverting my attention.

***

As the shuttle van drove through my gates, the driver whistled, "This is some estate."

"Yes, it is. The older I get, the more I appreciate it." Actually, the poorer I got, the more I appreciated it.

To distract me from finances, I looked out the window as we traveled the tree-lined drive. I could see the two-story grand plantation style house at the end and a sense of calmness came over me. The stately home had three wings. The left was a servant's area below with entertainment areas above. The other side being the guest rooms downstairs and children's rooms upstairs. The center wing housed the main living areas on the lower level and master bedroom suite on the upper. Unseen from this viewpoint were the pool house and a two-bedroom basement apartment. I enjoyed being the youngest and most pampered of three children growing up in this home.

Horatio's crew was trimming the already immaculate landscaping. Horatio himself was planting mealycup sage in a deep purple, offset with lightly colored dusty millers, to transfer the landscaping of the courtyard to heat-tolerant plants for the late summer season.

The driver helped get my luggage into the house—a much needed treat after trekking through two international airports and Waco's own regional terminal with my suitcases, a carry on, and an accessory bag in tow. I made a mental note to start packing lighter.

The first thing I did, after tipping the nice gentleman, was change into my swimsuit and exercise in the pool. I hadn't had the opportunity for weeks because of a broken arm and its accompanying cast courtesy of my second kidnapping of the summer season.

A flood of frustration released from my body with every stroke as I thought about my current circumstances. After my workout, I realized there wasn't a reason for me to feel guilty. Regardless of how things turned out, I truly had good intentions when marrying Sticks.

I went to bed feeling more relaxed than I had in a long time.

Until the noises started.

Chapter Four
An Impromptu Reunion

There they were again. I could hear a faint thumping followed by a sliding noise. I reached into my nightstand drawer and heard the loose bullets roll along the bottom. I scooped them up while grabbing my revolver and loaded it as quietly as I could, while chastising myself about not going to the shooting range this last week—or the last month. *God, if I get out of this alive, I promise to go to target practice.*

Climbing out of bed, I cursed the fact I had on my previously unworn wedding night attire to mourn the implosion of my marriage.

Soundlessly moving down the short hall to the family living area, I walked toward the kitchen, taking the last few steps with my back against the wall. A small beam of light could be seen floating through the room.

My breathing was heavy from fear as I listened to someone ransacking the kitchen. I reached around the wall and felt for the kitchen light, flipping it on as I swung into the entrance with my gun drawn.

A scream rent the air.

It was my high school nemesis, Roxanne. The last

time I saw her, we had made a kind-of truce. However, truces ended in the middle of the night under circumstances that could be considered breaking and entering.

To make matters worse, she was in an outfit like mine. Hers was a slutty red, whereas mine was virginal white though.

"What the hell are you doing here?" A perfectly reasonable question, which would have been more reasonable had it come from me.

"What do you mean, what am I doing here?" I put my gun on the counter to make sure I wouldn't accidentally shoot her on purpose then moved close enough to reach out and grab her hair. Somehow, I managed to restrain myself. "This is my house."

"Freeze!"

Both Roxanne and I screamed that time. Dylan, who was Cade's little brother, Sticks's subordinate, and a guy I had dated a few times, was standing in the kitchen entryway, wearing only boxers, pointing his gun at us. He must have been staying over with my best friend, Marsha. She was residing in the servant's quarters of the house while her condo was being renovated.

A loud thumping could be heard as someone thudded up the stairs. Rad, my ex-boyfriend from high school, emerged through the door leading to the basement apartment. He was dressed in a Speedo with handcuffs wrapped in a red boa hanging from one of his wrists. That explained why Roxanne was in my kitchen. But why had Rad been in the basement?

"What happened?" he asked breathlessly as he tucked his gun behind him, in a place I am positive I did not want to know. "Is everyone okay?"

"I was until I saw you in that. What are you doing in my house?"

"Didn't Marsha tell you? I rented the basement apartment. Mops was concerned about the hours I was keeping. She doesn't need me home now with Pops in the care facility and if I'm here, she can't keep track and won't worry." Rad was a detective for the Waco Police Department and had recently moved back to town. He was playing on my sympathy for his grandparents.

"Are you sure it wasn't the company you were keeping?" I asked, my gaze on Rad despite hearing the gasp of indignation from Roxanne.

I wanted to be mad at Marsha but couldn't. I needed the money and was sure she made him sign a lease at a premium price. I had been avoiding her since I had gotten married. Maybe she had had her own reasons for not speaking to me as well. She knew I wouldn't be happy with this news.

"For future reference, the basement apartment does not include my kitchen."

We were all distracted by the opening of the front door.

"You didn't lock that?" Rad accused as he reached behind him for his gun. "You've been kidnapped twice in the last two months."

"But not from my home."

Dylan also had his gun at-the-ready. I only

reached for my pink-handled .38 snubnose—which seemed exceptionally dainty compared to the firepower the men were carrying—because Roxanne was going for it.

"Please, Lainee, mine is downstairs. Besides, I'm a better shot than you."

I ignored her plea.

The light shone on a male form as he walked into the kitchen.

I inwardly groaned. How had my solitary pity party become an impromptu reunion?

"Definitely not how I pictured greeting my wife tonight," Sticks said as he leaned against the doorframe and surveyed all those gathered in the kitchen.

"Wife?" Dylan and Rad said in unison.

I held out my left hand, showing them my ring. "Yes, I am now Mrs. Clint Torres."

Rad started laughing.

"You think my marriage is a joke?" I accused.

Rad looked at everyone. "Come on, I couldn't have been the only one who got that." He paused. "Female body part?" Still no response. "Guys, say his name fast ten times. Clint Torres." Then he turned to Sticks. "You must not know enough to back up that name or you wouldn't have had to marry her. There are plenty of other ways to get her to unbuckle that Bible belt."

Sticks remained silent, arms crossed over his chest, confident and feeling no need to defend himself on his seduction skills.

Rad stood, ridiculously smug for someone who was wearing a Speedo, until Roxanne reacted to his statement. I enjoyed seeing his smile wane as the red palm mark across his cheek brightened.

Hilda rushed through the sunroom door from the pool house accompanied by her favorite frying pan raised high and ready to inflict bodily harm. She was spouting almost unintelligible words in her thickest Irish accent. "Why were there screams? Helga is calling 9-1-1." Hilda stopped short when she saw everyone and their attire. "Oh, dear." Her hand went to her robe pocket—a gesture I knew meant she was reaching for her rosary—only to come up empty. Instead, she crossed herself and left the room as quickly as she had entered.

Rad followed a pouting Roxanne out and said, "Roxanne, honey! I didn't mean anything by that."

Dylan asked, "Does Cade know?"

I shook my head.

He walked out, mumbling, "I don't know how I'm going to tell Marsha." I felt it was best to let her tell him she already knew.

That left Sticks and me to clean up the strawberries, chocolate sauce, and vegetable oil Roxanne had left on the counter, when Hilda came back to cleanse the area by sprinkling holy water.

Chapter Five
Whims

After Hilda left, Sticks and I went down the hall to my bedroom suite, which used to be the guest suite. Growing up, all the family bedrooms were upstairs with balconies that enjoyed views of the secluded peninsula of Lake Waco. I had to close those rooms, along with the media and game rooms, to save on expenses.

Sticks pulled off his suit jacket and placed it over the wingback chair in the sitting area by the bay window, then tiredly fell into the seat. "Between my mother's berating, the exhausting travel arrangements, the welcoming committee when I arrived, and Hilda's evil eye—which I have no idea why it was directed at me because I was the only fully clothed person on scene—along with having to meet with the DA early tomorrow…" He glanced at his watch. "No, this morning, I can't believe I'm going to pass up acting on the thoughts I had when I first saw you in that outfit."

"Good, because I'm thinking about burning it after seeing Roxanne's alternate version." I walked into the adjoining bathroom with my trusted ragged t-shirt and Soffe shorts which were my usual nighttime attire.

I returned to the bedroom, glad Sticks was there, even more so since he had stripped down to only his boxer briefs. He had piled the pillows against the headboard, his dark hair in contrast to the white pillowcases, and laid on top of the down comforter. I was having difficulty believing the man lounging on my bed was my husband. His skin was smooth with a natural tan and his build was bulky without an ounce of fat. Any woman would be proud to have him as a husband. So, other than the fact I didn't really know him, I couldn't think of a single reason to let him go. And to be honest, even that reason didn't cross my mind at the time.

I got in bed beside him but under the covers. "I'm sorry I told your mother that her English should be much better."

"Is that what you thought you said? Where did you learn to speak Spanish?"

"Horatio's foreman used to yell that at his workers. Horatio told me that's what it meant."

He smiled. "You may want to get another translation."

I took out my phone and looked it up. "Oh, my gosh." That was definitely not what I had said. I covered my face with both hands. "And Father Nelson was there, too."

Father Nelson had been summoned to the breakfast table the morning after I met Sticks's parents. Sticks and I were supposed to have met with him for the following two weeks—both of us for marriage counseling, then me by myself for Catechism classes. We only made it three days before Father insisted we tell Sticks's parents the truth. I wish he hadn't agreed to be there when we told them. He was a very nice man who should not have had to hear such vulgarities.

"It's alright. I haven't seen my dad laugh that hard in a long time."

"Did your mom ever come around to the idea of being a grandparent?"

That was the reason Sticks and I decided to get married. No, I wasn't pregnant. While attending his fifteen-year reunion, he realized his high school sweetheart had been harboring a very big secret. When he went to find out more information, she had disappeared, along with his daughter.

After visiting a lawyer to see what rights he had, Sticks had the idea to get engaged so he could have a better chance at getting custody by showing he could provide a stable home environment. It had been my idea to go ahead and get married.

"My mom kicked me out for bringing shame on the household by having an illegitimate child. I'm glad we didn't get around to telling her we got married for custody reasons. At least she doesn't know I'm in a marriage of convenience. I've never seen her so upset, and I shouldn't have asked you to put up with her behavior."

"We'll call it even, if you agree to put up with Hilda."

"I'm willing to try." His head fell back, and he

closed his eyes as he sighed. "What are we going to do about our little arrangement, Lainee? Do you want to end this?"

I reached out, interlacing my fingers through his. "No. Now that I'm away from your mother, I think we can make it work."

He sat up and crisscrossed his legs. My hand fell to his thigh. "Good, because the private investigator I hired may have found something useful."

I tilted my head and glared. "Let me get this straight. You hired a private investigator when your wife is a private investigator? Did you not think I could handle it?"

I could feel the muscles in Sticks's body tense as he weighed his next words carefully. "Lainee, I contacted him before we got married. I wasn't sure if you'd go through with the plan. Plus, he's in Arizona." He looked hopeful that I would forgive him. When I didn't, he got out his phone. "Look, I'll fix it. I'll e-mail and tell him he's no longer needed."

I covered his phone with my hand. "I watched your dad cater to your mother's every wish and now you're doing the same with me. There are times you're going to have to say no to my whims."

He smiled. "You realize if I don't e-mail him now, I'll be catering to your whim?"

"No, not really. A whim is more fanciful. This is logical. We need everything we can get on Meredith and Caitlynn, so someone needs to be out there searching. That reminds me." I reached over to get my laptop and opened it, showing Sticks a list of names.

"How did you come up with this?"

"I had to do something while I was being held prisoner by your parents and having to stay, by myself, in your old room. Also, I may have taken advantage of your statement to make myself at home. I looked through your yearbook and class reunion program." To justify my intrusion on his privacy, I added, "They were right out in the open."

"Yes, on my desk, under the box of mementos from high school."

"Exactly," I stated, neither confirming nor denying the fact that I may have also scoured the notes, photos, and keepsakes from his relationship with Meredith contained in said box. "I noticed several snapshots of Meredith with Jessica and Naomi. Their full names were under their senior pictures, so I listed various combinations of all of them." People typically hold on to parts of their past when they start over. I felt Meredith wouldn't have strayed far in her new name choice. "Then when I got home this evening, I ran the names through my software. Look at the one I highlighted. She has a daughter whose birthday is a date that holds significance to both Meredith and you."

"The day of our prom," he said, looking over the list again. "Very impressive, Lainee."

"Speaking of Jessica and Naomi, do they have any ideas about where Meredith went?"

"They were as surprised as I was that she took off. Naomi mentioned Meredith had sat down with Caitlynn the day after our reunion and told her about me. Then Jessica mentioned it caused a huge argument with her husband and Caitlynn didn't handle the news well either. Everyone agreed Meredith regretted letting her secret out."

"Have you spoken with the husband?"

"Yes. I went by his office when I couldn't reach Meredith. He's a lawyer out in Arizona. Still the same cocky asshole he was back in the day. Always getting into trouble, but his parents bailed him out."

"You knew him from before? Did Meredith?"

"Yes, we all knew each other. Graduated from the same school. He's a few years older though. We competed against each other on the wrestling team. Both in the same weight class. Chapped him I was on his level at a younger age."

"Do you think he could be Caitlynn's father?"

"No, not at all. Meredith and I were each other's firsts. We planned on getting married, but after graduation she cut off all contact. I know now it was because she had told her parents she was pregnant, and they threatened her if she told me. At the time, I thought it was because she was upset I went into the military and she didn't want that type of life. She didn't marry Brad until years later. Again, at the insistence of her parents. They loved the idea of her marrying into a wealthy family and being a corporate lawyer's wife."

"What did he say when you spoke to him?"

He leaned against the headboard. "The interview went all over the place. First, he was mad, said he thought she'd run off with me. Tried to bow up but caved pretty quick. Then he acted nonchalant, like she'd be back soon and there was nothing to worry about. Finally, he showed concern. Broke down in tears, for God's sake. All I know is something was off. I wish I would have gotten it on video, but I went over there as a concerned friend. He definitely knows more than what he's saying but it's nothing I can prove. Yet."

"Maybe he was nervous that someone from the FBI was speaking to him. Do you think he felt guilty because he's done something to them? Or she might have asked him to cover for her."

"It could have been a lot of things, Lainee. We can't piece it together at this point. We do know both his and her ATM cards were used to take out the daily maximum on the day she left and that she got a cash advance on a credit card. There's been no cell phone usage and all transactions on her debit card show she was traveling west on Interstate 10. The trail goes cold after two days. That's all the PI has been able to gather."

"Why would she use her debit card if she had cash? My gut tells me she faked a trail then retraced her route and headed east."

"Makes sense, but you never know how someone reacts to being on the run. Especially someone like Meredith who is used to having every convenience. It could have simply been out of habit or she may have wanted to save the cash for when she got closer to her destination. I am so tempted to use FBI resources to find them but need everything to be above board in order to get any custody rights."

"You're right. I've been thinking about how we should disclose the information we find. You hiring the other investigator may be the answer. We can feed him our leads. The same reason you can't use any of your FBI contacts is the same reason you shouldn't hire me. We don't want Meredith to say we abused our power or gathered intelligence unlawfully. It would taint our chances in court for getting custody."

"I like the way my wife thinks." He leaned sideways onto his elbow and tried to close the distance between us, but I straight-armed him.

"You shouldn't confuse me being reasonable with me no longer being mad."

"Wait. I thought we decided the second PI was a good thing."

"We did, but I'm still angry that you didn't ask to hire me first. Now, let's get to bed."

His eyes twinkled as if there was hope things might progress physically.

I extinguished it. Twisting around to turn off my lamp, I said, "To go to sleep, Clint."

"You sound like my mother when you call me Clint." He got up, grabbed the grooming kit from his luggage and went into the bathroom. I heard the toilet flush then water running in the sink. He opened the door and stuck his head through with a toothbrush hanging from his mouth. "Hey, what if I said no to your whim of going to sleep right away?"

I glared at him.

He smiled and raised his eyebrows. "What about

maybe? What if I said maybe to your whim?"

Despite the charm of him looking as if he were frothing from the mouth, I rolled over, turning my back to him.

Eventually, he crawled into bed, stayed on his own side, and did nothing but sleep.

Chapter Six
No Perks

As I stretched before my jog the next morning, Marsha walked up and lounged on the garden bench. She looked relaxed. Her long blonde hair was haphazardly styled into a messy bun. She wore a plain white t-shirt and boxer shorts—what looked to be the same ones Dylan was wearing the previous night—which emphasized her tanned, muscular legs that were never-ending.

"Dylan told me you saw Rad last night. I guess I can stop avoiding you now." She took a sip of coffee, then gave me a large manila envelope. "Here's the lease agreement. You'll need to sign it and give a copy to Rad for it to be official."

"Hallelujah! There's still a chance I can evict him." My morning was looking brighter.

"You may want to look over the terms first."

I opened the envelope and scanned the paperwork.

"Holy moly," was the only statement I could muster. Marsha had gouged him on the rent. I would have to substitute teach six weeks to get the same amount of money.

Quickly signing the documents before weighing all of the pros and cons, I sat them on the bench and picked up on Marsha's earlier statement. "Since when do you avoid situations? That's my pattern of behavior. I thought you were blowing me off my first night back in town to go out with Dylan before he left for the weekend." Even though Dylan was an FBI agent, he chose to let most people think his sole source of income was stripping every weekend at a club outside of Fort Worth. I only found out about his more honorable employment after I was taken hostage and Dylan was on the team of rescuers.

"That's basically what happened. Would it make you feel better to know Dylan was also blown off?" Marsha smirked. "Much different context though."

Even though I enjoyed morning jogs through my landscaped five-acre estate, I decided to do a modified yoga workout instead of running so Marsha could fill in the details of her story.

I was enjoying the conversation until she asked, "How is married life treating you? You know this is quid pro quo. You have to share your details, too."

"Unfortunately, I don't have any details to share."

"What?" She literally set aside her precious caffeinated beverage and sat up. "Why did you get married then? I thought it was because of your new encounter system." She looked dumbfounded. "So, the period of silence wasn't because you were enjoying the benefits of marriage?"

I explained the situation in Arizona to her.

"Well, what about last night? Dylan said Sticks

came in and announced you guys were married."

"We had a slight argument."

"You're deflating my ego, Lainee. If an argument stopped you from having sex, then I haven't been doing a good enough job describing my make-up sex adventures to you." She picked up her phone and began texting.

"You know it's rude to text in the middle of a conversation. What's so important?"

"I'm picking a fight with Dylan to provide new learning material." Marsha turned to me. "Oh, don't look so shocked. You should be appreciative. I'm making a sacrifice for you."

"Doing things you enjoy is not a sacrifice."

The deeper into this conversation we got, the more difficult it was to stay balanced in my poses. I was beginning to regret not jogging as Marsha lectured me on the advantages of a healthy sex life and the detriments of being a maiden.

"I'll admit when I pushed to get married, I was thinking about guilt-free relations any time I wanted. But I'm glad when there's a reason not to go through with the big bang. It feels wrong, almost like we're about to go all the way on a first date, even though we're married. You do remember Sticks and I haven't been on a date yet?"

"The word you're sidestepping is sex, Lainee, and there's something to be said about sex on first dates. You'd know if you'd ever try it."

"That's not really my style."

"Neither is running off and getting married."

"Technically, I didn't run off to get married. I ran off after I was married." I gave up on exercising and sat beside Marsha. "And I'm not doing well with my vows. I keep thinking about Cade, and, God help me, sometimes Rad, but I made the commitment and have to follow through."

"You're fine as long as you're just thinking and not doing."

"I'm not so sure. Cade is the perfect person for me. He has a steady job, wants to stay local, and I don't have to tell you about how good he looks." I took the towel and wiped some perspiration from my forehead. "Rad is an unfinished project. I see such good in him sometimes and feel like he's on the cusp of doing the right thing. I'm a good influence on him."

"But he's a bad influence on you."

"Don't be so judgmental, Marsha. You're a bad influence on me too." I swatted at an insect. "Bad feels so good with him, though."

She gave me a reproachful look.

"And when I think of my husband, there's a blank slate. It's nice to have this dream of a married life, but I don't have a vision of the future. Where would we live? Would he quit his job to live here? There isn't an FBI field office here. Does he want children? Is he a Catholic or just going through the motions to please his mother? I have no clue about what a life with him would be like." I also didn't know how I was going to disengage myself from this facade of a marriage once the case was over.

"Here's what I'm hearing. Cade is your safety

line, Rad is your bad boy, and Sticks is the unknown. And here's what I know. It's a bit too late to give you the advice that I think you should hear. So, all I can tell you at this point is that you really need to let Cade know that you're married soon."

"I'm sure he'll find out today, but I thought I'd have more time to prepare." Cade was a teacher and coach at a local middle school. We met when I had a long-term substituting position there. "Today's my first day back. Mrs. Goodson had her baby earlier than expected, and I'll be working across the hall from him for four weeks."

"If you don't let him know, Dylan will. He wanted to call Cade last night, but I managed to distract him."

"Yes, I heard about your distraction techniques earlier." I slumped. "Being married is more difficult than I planned. What should I do?"

She sat quietly, staring at birds playing in the nearby fountain.

"Are you giving me the silent treatment because you're mad at me for getting married?"

"Of course, I'm mad about it, Lainee. You're putting me in the position of being the sensible one in our friendship. But I'm not saying anything because I can't help you if you won't tell me what's really going on." She finally looked at me. "Honestly, if it wasn't about sex and the stupid rules you make up in order to have it, why did you do it?"

It was my turn to find the birds interesting. Sticks and I agreed not to tell anyone why we got married. We wanted everyone to treat us naturally.

Unfortunately, most people were standoffish or downright hostile to couples who had married after knowing each other only a few weeks.

When it became obvious I wasn't going to answer, Marsha tipped her mug, drank the remainder of her coffee, and got up. "It's hard to be supportive of this. Besides, you know I'm cranky until after my second cup." As she walked into the house, she added, "Sounds like you have a decision to make, but I wouldn't come to a conclusion before experiencing all the perks."

Left alone with my jumbled thoughts, I went ahead with my run to clear my head.

Chapter Seven
Explanations

Cade walked into the classroom and looked at my name on the board. "So it's true then. Mrs. Delaney-Torres. I thought Kyle was lying when he told me." He stood completely still, staring at the name. "When did it happen?"

"About a week ago."

He inhaled deeply, then exhaled sharply while pinching the bridge of his nose. "Right after you found Rachel and me together."

Rachel was his ex-fiancée. Cade and I were on a relationship break when I decided to surprise him with the news I wanted to start dating again. Needless to say, I was the one bowled over when I got to his apartment that morning.

"Who's Mr. Torres? I thought Rad's last name was Thorpe."

Conrad Bartholomew Thorpe, III, also known as Rad, the indelicate ex-high school boyfriend who was now my tenant, was the reason I couldn't be too judgmental of Cade. During our break, I had a momentary indiscretion as well, which indirectly led me on the path to marriage. There were some twists and turns along the way, but the journey led to my newly developed intimacy plan that was designed to help minimize making any further out-of-wedlock mistakes. Sticks cut through all the red tape and asked me to marry him, along with helping him get his daughter back. It seemed like a win-win situation at the time.

"You remember Sticks? The doctor who treated us?"

Cade nodded, then asked, "Lainee, why? I thought you would need some time to calm down. I hoped you'd let me explain everything today. You and I had put on the brakes and Rachel showed up the next day after almost two years. It just happened. When it was over, I felt nothing but regret. It wasn't fair to you or Rachel. I thought you would understand because I assumed you had the same type of experience with Rad in Galveston. Didn't you want to give us a second chance when you came over that morning?" He paced to the other side of the room then abruptly turned. "God, you weren't going to tell me you were getting married, were you?"

"Cade, it's a long, complicated story. I can only say it's not what it seems."

"It seems like you're married."

I sighed, "Then I guess it's exactly how it seems."

Without another word, he straightened to his full six-foot-one-inch height, turned his back to me, and left.

I sat at the desk, glued to the seat, at a loss as to what I should do. Going after him would only make matters worse. Never once did I think about the pain this sham would cause others. When I agreed to Sticks's engagement plan, then escalated it to my marriage plan, I did it to help him, not hurt Cade. That was the problem of not thinking things through.

I resumed reading the teacher's instructions, but my thoughts drifted to the night Sticks asked me to marry him. To say I had just had a horrible, ego-depleting day would be understating the situation. After walking in on the aftereffects of Cade comforting his ex-fiancée, I left that scene only to witness Rad preparing to tell his grandparents about his relationship with Roxanne. On the drive home, I had tried to soothe my misery with chocolates, but it was finding Sticks in my kitchen helping Hilda cook that had softened the double blow.

Excusing ourselves to a more private location, then me jumping Sticks in a very unladylike manner mollified my mood even more. The single most alleviating factor for my overwrought condition though, was when he got down on one knee, pulled out a ring, and proposed marriage.

When my senses returned, I stammered, "M-maybe I was too adamant about my rules for intimate physical ventures. Y-you don't really have to ask me to marry you. We can go back, yes, let's go back to the ten-to-one ratio guidelines." That plan had been my last attempt to concede to my libido while still trying to maintain my honor. It was based on the theory that I shouldn't count the partners I accepted. Instead, I should tally the ones rejected. Once I had denied ten, I could then choose any one of them.

In my defense, it had seemed more logical the previous week.

"You've faced a double agent, a mob boss, and, if news reports are to be trusted, a stalker-turned-killer, but I've never seen you this scared." He chuckled. "I only asked you to marry me." Sticks stood, placed his hands on my shoulders, and gently guided me backward, then down into one of the wingback chairs. "Take deep breaths. Inhale. Exhale." He modeled a few for me before saying, "Let's look at the bigger picture. Before you attacked me, which I thoroughly enjoyed by the way, remember I asked you to help me with a case? We should start there."

Sticks started there, but we finished at the Justice of the Peace's office the next afternoon.

The school bell rang, interrupting my thoughts, as I scrambled to get ready for the students.

Each class period, I compared the students to Sticks's daughter. She would be two years older than them. I wondered what she would look like. I had seen the prom picture of Meredith and the teenage Clint. If Meredith had been telling the truth about the parentage, Caitlynn would have been conceived only hours after that photo was taken.

Sticks had looked the same as he did now. The only differences were in his expression. His smile was more relaxed then and the crease in his forehead that gave the illusion of a permanent scowl had not yet developed. For an eighteen-year-old, he had already begun to fill out with a broad chest and athletic build.

His darker skin directly contrasted Meredith's fair, almost porcelain-perfected complexion. His crew cut dark hair was barely noticeable, whereas Meredith's was the main feature. Her strawberry blond locks were pulled up in front and left to flow in full curls in back.

According to genetic dominance laws, his daughter would probably have his dark hair, eyes, and skin tone. However, with my fair, freckled skin from my dad's Irish family and long, straight black hair and brown eyes from my mom's American Indian ancestry, I was living proof genetics were unpredictable.

Chapter Eight
Taillights

After two weeks of marriage, I discovered Sticks's life was anything but long term. Dylan occasionally informed me of his boss's travel plans, which were many. He hadn't stayed in one area for more than three consecutive days and had only stayed in Waco that one night since I had returned from Arizona.

To fill the time during his absence, as well as pad my pocketbook since I was working for him free of charge, I decided to take on another case. The kind of case that was the bread and butter of most private investigator businesses. As I crouched in the bushes—which, by the smell, was used as a litter box by the neighborhood cat—while trying to position the listening device for the clearest reception, I was unsure if this evidence should be turned over to my client. His wife and so-called best friend were belittling him as a husband, lover, father, and businessman. No one needed to hear that about themselves.

Merely recording this conversation wasn't going to get his prenuptial agreement invalidated though. I had to prove infidelity. A task made more difficult by the fact I could only gather audio. The windows were covered, and I hadn't had time to plant surveillance equipment inside the house before my client had left town. I shouldn't have worried. The task was made easier by the loudness and descriptive vocabulary skills of the wife. She had missed her calling as a play-by-play sports announcer.

Shortly afterward, when I heard her complaining about the man getting dressed, I took the opportunity to move. Unfortunately, I had not factored in my legs falling asleep. Instead of standing, I fell and my equipment clanked as it scattered throughout the flower bed. The porch light immediately came on. That was good news. If they were already at the door, maybe they hadn't heard. I flattened myself against the wall as the adulterous couple said their goodbyes. I smiled. Lainee Luck was not failing me. I was going to come out of this unscathed.

At least that's what I thought until a light shown behind me. "Don't move. I've already called the police."

An impossibly old woman in a cotton nightgown put down her flashlight so she could steady the gun she had pointed at me. I remained still, unsure if the woman's shaky hands would accidentally pull the trigger.

I heard a car drive off as a second one with red and blue flashing lights approached. I simply raised my hands in the air waiting for an officer to rescue me from the woman who could be the Golden Girls' grandmother.

***

By stepping onto the running board and grasping the, for lack of a better term, 'oh-shit' handle, I was able to pull myself into Cade's truck.

"Why the hell did you call me?" Cade asked as he had easily lifted himself into the truck, no assistance needed.

"You are very snitty when you wake up in the middle of the night. I am thankful I have never seen this side of you before."

"Don't go getting your Southern-belle, manners-are-the-center-of-the-universe panties in a wad. There were plenty of other people you could have called to come haul your ass out of jail."

"I thank you for coming to get me, but I don't appreciate your language or your tone."

He started the truck and put it into gear. "Well, maybe you can recount your displeasure to your husband, who should have been your first choice to call. Then there's your ex-boyfriend who is on the police force and probably still inside the building. Hell, you could have even chosen my brother, who you also used to date."

If he hadn't been right about everything else, I might have corrected his grammar. It was *whom I also used to date*.

Traffic was light as he pulled onto the street. "Once you ran out of ex-boyfriends, you could have called Marsha."

He made my life sound so tawdry. Why had I called him? It took me a moment to remember. "I chose you because I thought you would be the person who would give me the least amount of grief. Evidently, I was mistaken."

Cade slid into his logical mode, his speech becoming slow and deliberate. "You think I'll give you the least amount of grief because I'm the person who matters least in your life."

"That isn't true." I meekly argued. But it was. I had chosen him to come to the rescue because he was my backup plan.

My expression must have shown my realization.

"Don't say anything else," he said. "I can't bear to hear it."

We were silent until Cade pulled into the circular driveway in front of my home, which gave me enough time to realize what I was really doing. Despite the rationalizations I contrived for marrying Sticks, Cade knew none of them. He didn't know that I was conflicted about my feelings for the men in my life. To him, I simply tossed him aside until I needed to use him again.

I opened the door slightly and paused, turning to him. "Thanks, Cade."

He continued to stare straight ahead. "I can't help you out anymore, Lainee. It only gives me hope when there isn't any."

I got out of the truck, watched as his taillights faded from view, and wiped a tear away.

Chapter Nine
Moment of Insanity

To keep my nose clean for the next few days, I settled into a routine of exercise, work, and sleep, with the occasional phone call to or from my defense attorney.

My routine was broken when someone startled me awake. That had not been the safest avenue for this person to travel. Scratching the first thing I found with one hand, while reaching for the mug of chamomile tea on my night stand and swinging with the other, I was able to inflict a fair amount of pain before I recognized the intruder was my husband.

"Oh, my! Sticks, I'm sorry, but what are you doing, coming into my room in the middle of the night?"

"If you hadn't been avoiding my calls and texts, you'd know exactly what I was doing. I'm in town for the Bellagio case and will be gone before you get up this morning. I was letting you know I made it in safely."

"I wasn't avoiding your texts and calls." I rubbed his shoulder where my mug had landed.

He seemed unconvinced of the truth of my

statement as I walked to the *en suite* to get alcohol swabs and a bandage for the scratch on his forearm. I had married an intelligent man but one who had a lack of understanding when it came to Lainee Logic.

When I returned, I clarified for him. "I didn't receive any texts or calls, and since there was no correspondence from you, you did not meet my three-to-one guideline for suitors. Hence, my reason for not contacting you."

Sticks sighed. "For God's sake, Lainee, I'm not your suitor, I'm your husband, and I contacted you every day." He got out his phone and tapped a few buttons. "Let's see. I texted you again."

We both looked at my phone waiting for the notification beep. Nothing happened.

"I did text you." He showed me the messages he had sent.

I scrolled through them. "This one is sweet, thank you." Then further down. "Now here, you're starting to get rude."

"One tends to do that when they're being ignored."

"I told you, I wasn't ignoring you." I grabbed my phone. "Look. No messages from you."

"I see plenty from Cade."

"That's because he walks the other way every time he sees me."

"I don't see that as a problem."

"You aren't factoring in he's the lead social studies teacher, and I need to get information about what I'm supposed to teach each day. We have to communicate somehow."

Sticks squinted at the screen as he scrolled through the messages. "Wait. What is this one? *Thanks for getting me out of jail.*" He mouthed the words again, knowing what they meant but asking the question anyway. "What does that mean?"

I briefly thought about lying. When I was a little girl, I remembered a fundraiser where the principal was locked in a make-shift jail on campus until enough money was raised to get him out. Then another prominent community or school leader would be sentenced. That was a feasible lie. It would work. If I didn't have to explain why I would have to be appearing in court in a few weeks.

I decided to go with the truth. "I got arrested for trespassing when I was working on a case. My lawyer thinks it will be dismissed because I had permission from the husband to be on the property. It's nothing to worry about. I don't think it will affect custody proceedings."

Sticks wasn't distracted by the custody comment. "So, Cade was the person you called? What about Marsha or Hilda?"

"Hilda? Are you serious?" Why was everyone concerned about my choices lately? This was just one more I had made when I wasn't thinking clearly.

"I see your point. But you're not seeing mine. Cade is not the person you should think about when you're in trouble."

"It wasn't like I knew where you were."

"Again. Not my fault. I don't know why you

weren't receiving my texts."

"Wait a minute." I walked over to my chest of drawers and pulled out my work phone.

The battery was dead, so I had to plug it in to turn it on. Sure enough, there were several texts, not only from Sticks but also from his team members from weeks ago wanting to know how I was feeling.

"You were texting the wrong number. You have the one I use when I'm undercover."

"You call your ex-boyfriend when you need help, and I, your husband, don't have your number. Do you realize how insane all of this is?"

"Well, by definition, insanity is where a person can't distinguish the difference between right or wrong, or reality from fantasy." I walked to the bathroom to throw away the bandage packaging, speaking louder so he could hear. "Therefore, if I realized my actions were insane, they wouldn't be insane. It's a catch twenty-two."

When I returned, he had moved to the loveseat. "Why are you rubbing your temples, Sticks? Do you have a headache? I can get some ibuprofen."

He stood and started unbuttoning his dress shirt, removing it to expose his muscular chest beneath.

"No need," he said, shaking his head. "I'm just tired."

I enjoyed the scene, watching his muscles flex as he moved to lift and unzip his garment bag, then hang a second suit in the smaller of the two closets in my room where Hilda had emptied a space for him earlier in the week for the rare occasion that he might stay over.

He turned abruptly, more unamused than before, as he placed both hands on his hips. "You need to clear your calendar tonight because we're having dinner so we can talk things out."

"Don't you think you should ask a lady to dinner? You're being presumptuous. I've got a long day ahead and already made plans with Hilda and Helga for this evening. I don't want to cancel them because Hilda finally spoke nicely to me yesterday." Earlier communication had been through terse comments or scathing facial expressions. "Evidently, she was more upset about the kitchen incident than I thought."

"Hilda, unlike you, has been talking to me. Your plans with them was her way of getting us together. She was prepared to either track you down or tie you down, whatever it took for us to talk."

He was now putting the rest of the items from his overnight bag in his solitary drawer and walked to the adjoining bathroom to get ready for bed.

When he came out, I said, "I don't like people making plans for me, especially on short notice."

Sticks climbed into bed. "You don't like plans at all recently."

"You're wrong. I love plans. I make lists and lists of plans. I just haven't been following through with any lately." I snuggled close and wiggled invitingly.

He grabbed my hip, putting a halt to my offer. "You shouldn't confuse me being reasonable with me not being mad."

I inwardly groaned. I hated when my words were

used against me.

He turned over. "It's going to be a long day. We need to get some sleep."

Chapter Ten
A Better Proposition

When I got home, Hilda was directing Horatio as he strung lights in the sunroom. I could only imagine what theme she was staging for my dinner with Sticks that evening. She shooed me away and banned me to my room until everything was ready.

I was carried back to my childhood when she brought in a pitcher of lemonade and a tray of fresh fruits, placing them on the coffee table, then saying, "Here's an after-school snack for you." The flashback was ruined when she added, "But you have to save some for Agent Torres." I felt guilty as I realized she was putting more effort into making my marriage work than I was.

I sat on the loveseat and pulled papers out of my tote to grade. Sticks was ushered into the room an hour and a half later. He mimicked the scene from his unexpected arrival early that morning by putting his keys in the corner of his one small drawer and getting out a hanger for his tie and jacket. If this was going to work, I needed to make more room for him in my home—and my life. Putting the papers aside, I asked, "How was your day?"

"Not so good. Marcus's lawyer is wanting you to support their self-defense claim."

Marcus Bianchini was previously one of the men under Sticks's command. He had also been taking orders from Mario Bellagio, the kingpin of Chicago's mafia. Marcus had escorted me, in the cramped confines of his trunk, to a slaughter house with the intent to kill me. In the name of all things ironic, I wound up saving his life.

"Marcus did shoot in self-defense, but how are they planning to explain my presence? He would have to admit to kidnapping me."

"He said you got into the trunk on your own to hide during his meeting with Mr. Bellagio."

"Only if he means on my own because he was pointing a gun at me."

"I can guarantee the prosecution will present that during the trial. The District Attorney will want to meet to go over possible questions. You have to know his defense team will portray you as an accomplice who was wanting in on the action. Marcus is saying that he spoke with you the night he placed the photo of Paul on your pillow and you agreed to meet with him at the ranch to get the flashdrive."

"That's not true!"

"We know that, Lainee. We simply have to convince the jury."

Thinking about how Paul looked with the small, round red hole through his forehead was something I had repressed. "I don't want to relive all of this."

Sticks stepped toward me. Closing my eyes, I put

my hands up, not wanting him near me. I needed to get my memories under control. *Take calming breaths. Focus on the present. Crime lords and testimonies move to the back. Newlywed business owner and educator come to the forefront. Now cleansing breaths.* I was ready.

When I opened my eyes, Sticks had untucked his shirt and was sitting in the wingback chair across from me. I gave him a nod and he continued. "I also need to talk about what's happening in Chicago. The turf wars are abating. With them no longer fighting to see who'll come out on top, they're looking for vengeance. We've stepped up our security of Marcus since he's going to testify against others in the organization, but you don't have that bargaining tool. The fact that, even though you didn't kill Bellagio, you did shoot him, may make you a target."

Part of me saving Marcus's life was also shooting Mr. Bellagio in the stomach. It hindered him enough for Marcus to reach a gun and finish the crime lord off with a shot to the head.

"When will all of this occur? I just made it to long-term substitute status. If it happens during this assignment, not only will I lose pay for the days I'm off, but I'll also lose the pay-grade difference."

"You're not getting it." He moved beside me on the couch. "You could lose a lot more than money. The bottom line is you're on the front line. I don't want to be a widow, Lainee."

He shifted quickly and kissed me. I briefly thought I should tell him he would be a widow*er*, but that one kiss released the quelled desire of every night spent away from each other. It also alleviated much of the frustration built from the nights spent together but worlds apart. Soon grammar was no longer on my mind.

Actually, I was giving the kiss too much credit. It was also the weight of him against me as he gently guided us to lie on the cramped loveseat. Added to that was the pressure of his thigh between mine hinting for a better proposition. One of his hands ran through my hair as the other was becoming well-acquainted with my left breast.

I was finally starting to like the married life. Which I'm sure was the reason Hilda chose that moment to knock and tell us dinner was ready.

Sticks leaned his forehead against mine. "I'm going to be a little late for dinner."

"Sorry to leave you in this situation again." And me. Even though my wants weren't as obviously projecting themselves, they remained unfulfilled as well.

"It's like I'm reliving my high school days," he said.

I slid from underneath him and sat up, running my fingers through my hair to straighten it. "Let's pick up where we left off after dinner."

"Can't. I'm meeting with WPD later this evening. Not sure when, or if, I'll make it in." He stretched his leg and pulled at the crease of his pants to attempt a covert adjustment, then continued. "This is a quick trip. Heading to Chicago in the morning."

"Do you realize I don't know what you look like when you first wake up?"

"Yes. Do you realize I like watching you sleep before I start my day?"

I leaned over and kissed him again.

He put both hands on my shoulders and pushed me away. "You're going to have to go out there before Hilda comes in. I'm not sure either of us would want to deal with that."

Chapter Eleven
Dinner for Two?

Hilda had made pan seared salmon with thyme-roasted carrots in brown sugar, butter, and caper sauce. I loved eating Hilda's cooking but was always nervous when she cooked for a suitor. I knew they would be severely disappointed if I ever prepared a meal for them. Of course, as Sticks had previously pointed out, he was not my suitor.

String lights were interspersed through the faux ivy vines draping from every available surface in the sunroom. The blinds were opened to the view of the swimming pool that had lily pads boasting votive candles floating throughout. The theme of ivy and string lights was echoed under the cabana, creating a romantic setting.

Sticks took a sip of his wine. "This is a beautiful house, Lainee. Does it ever seem overwhelming being here on your own?"

"I'm not really on my own. I've always had Hilda, now Helga, too. And Horatio checks in at least once a week before doing a gardening project. Although, I have to admit it's been hard since my parents died."

"I read the cause was carbon monoxide

poisoning."

"Yes, it was a minor auto accident. They slid off the road during a snow storm. Their car wasn't even damaged. It happened because their tail pipe was covered by a snow drift as they waited for the tow truck to arrive. I have always regretted not going to get them."

My parents had been lively people who enjoyed one another and all life had to offer. All of their assets had been divided evenly between my siblings and me. The difference being their boon was income generating whereas mine was income depleting. My brother, Alvin, received the law firm. My sister, Florence or Flo for short, took over the art studio. Both also inherited rental properties. I got the house.

"Before their deaths, I'd never had to pay bills or watch what I spent."

"You've adapted to your financial situation well. It's not all about the money though. You've made sacrifices to ensure the staff doesn't have to worry about losing their employment, all while starting a business from scratch and taking on a second job to make sure the bills get paid. It shows resilience and I think your parents would be proud of you, Lainee."

"Thank you." His words were more comforting than I would have thought. I had been fighting the perception of being a spoiled rich girl. From an outsider's view, I still had it all. Not many could see that none of the expectations I had for my life were being met by my current circumstances, nor were they witness to the struggles I was facing.

"In my mind, I thought their deaths would happen much later in my life and never both of them together. I envisioned my brother sorting the estate neatly in the background while I continued to carpool my children and plan parties for my husband's business ventures."

Sticks used his napkin to wipe a tear from my cheek.

"I guess reality had a different plan." I guided his hand to the table. Feeling embarrassed for crying in front of him, I straightened in my seat, reminding myself of dining etiquette and proper posture lessons from Grandma Elaine.

Sticks cleared his throat, attempting to return the conversation to a casual track. "Well, I had an unplanned reality, too. Although I like the curve—or curves, in this case—that it's thrown at me."

"Yes. Our marriage was definitely a curve ball and I think we should make it more official."

"I agree one hundred percent." He leaned across the table and kissed me.

I pulled away slightly. "I'm glad. I wasn't sure how much you'd want to be involved."

"Oh, I promise I'll be a very active participant," he said before kissing me again.

This time I pushed him away more forcefully. "We need to start planning right away then."

He sat back in his chair. "Timing is important, but I don't think every detail needs to be planned. Don't you think we could simply start then see where it leads?"

"That's not how we do it here in the South. There

has to be friends and family all around to help celebrate if it's going to be done correctly."

"I somehow don't think we're on the same page. Why don't you tell me what you're planning?"

"We need to have a reception. Helga can help arrange everything. She used to be an event organizer. We could have it here at the house. I can see it all now." I stood, walked to the windows, and gestured. "There would be plenty of space if we opened the French doors and used the patio. A band could set up between the cabana and pool house, tables would go in the lawn, and the cabana could double as a dance floor." Ignoring the fact that I was reminding myself of Hilda on one of her tirades, I continued. "We'd have to think of a theme. Let me know if you have any ideas. In case of inclement weather, we could use the game and media rooms upstairs. The house could accommodate a guest list of 100-150 people. How many do you think would attend from your side of the family?"

Sitting once again across from Sticks, I noticed he was speechless, probably second guessing his eagerness to make our marriage more official.

We were surprised by Rad walking through the kitchen and standing beside our table. He grabbed my glass of wine and drank it in one gulp. "I don't think you'll be needing this." Then he took a roasted carrot from my plate and ate it. "This tastes great, which means you didn't cook it, Lainee. Hubby must be better in the kitchen than in the bedroom."

I ignored his taunt. "What are you doing here?"

"I need to talk to Clint." I'm not sure, but I think he left the 'n' sound out of the name. When Sticks looked up but remained seated, Rad added, "Just between us, Agent."

The men moved to the corner and spoke in whispers.

Walking to me, Sticks placed a quick kiss on my cheek, "I have to cut dinner short. Something's come up."

Rad swung by the table as well and picked up the bottle of wine. "I'll take this and put it away in case you're tempted to drink alone."

I was left staring at the French doors as they exited to go to the police station.

Chapter Twelve
Injuries

I woke up to the sound of someone rummaging through the bathroom. Sticks's plans must have changed. I debated on whether I should get up and help or go back to sleep. After all, I had stayed up late discussing locations, menus, invitations, and other details of the reception with Helga, while Hilda played the part of the bride's overbearing mother well, interrupting with her own thoughts and suggestions. I went to sleep confident that Helga would take care of all the details. Now, groggily, and a bit grudgingly, I got out of bed to help my husband.

The source of the noise wasn't Sticks. It was Rad, shirtless but thankfully in pajama bottoms instead of a Speedo. I admired the way they hung low on his hips and briefly thought about what those powerful hips could do. Eventually, I remembered I was a married woman, tucked away all—well, at least most of—those lustful thoughts, and got upset he was going through my medicine cabinet and searching underneath my counters.

"What are you doing? I told you this area wasn't part of the apartment."

He still had his back to me. "Actually, your words

were 'the basement apartment does not include my kitchen.'"

"I thought you were intelligent enough to generalize the concept."

"I am intelligent enough." He turned, and I saw blue and purple bruising on his ribs.

"Oh, my gosh. What happened?"

"Lainee, I found it's best not to tell people who love me what happens in the line of duty."

"Then I don't see why you can't tell me."

"Don't be like that. Just because we didn't work out doesn't mean we don't love each other." He walked around me. "Sorry I woke you. I'm sure you need your rest, but since you're up, where do you keep your Ace bandages? My ribs are killing me."

I led him down the hallway to the kitchen and the fully stocked first aid kit in the service pantry.

"Do you really think this is the first time you should be telling me you love me? Wouldn't it have been more relevant when we were dating?"

"Maybe I didn't tell you then because I knew it would make your happily-ever-after fantasies crash harder when the inevitable happened." He was right. It was hard enough to give up our relationship in high school. If I'd known he loved me, I would have become the poster child for a clingy woman.

I found the elastic bandage and held it out to him. Instead of taking it, he raised his arms. "Would you mind wrapping my ribs?"

My pulse quickened. With our line of conversation, I was hesitant to get too close but knew he wouldn't be able to wrap them on his own.

"Back then, I didn't think I was going to be around for you. Now I see that's the type you go for. It's ironic your husband is always gone and I'm the one sleeping in the same house as you every night. I might have sold myself short."

I wound the bandage around his ribs, making my moves deliberate, not wanting to get too close. "You only want what you can't have, Rad."

He put a finger under my chin and stared into my eyes. "You're always wound so tight, Lainee. Sometimes I miss being the one who loosens you up. I know you miss it, too. What we did in Galveston proves it." He inched closer.

I responded by pulling at the bandages, possibly a tad bit too forcefully, making sure they were snug. Rad doubled over and gasped at the pain, breaking eye contact.

This time, I held my finger under his chin and lifted his head to make sure he got the message. "Sometimes isn't good enough for me, Rad. Galveston was a mistake."

"Agreed. We shouldn't have—how to put this to not offend your Southern sensibilities—had so much fun together, but not everything about that trip was a mistake. We learned how to work through our differences and that may come in handy soon."

"What we need to work on is you staying in your own area. And you need to remember, you may be sleeping in the same house as me, but most nights you sleep in the same bed as Roxanne." I started walking to my room. "The next time you need medical assistance, call her. Walgreen's is opened 24 hours. She can get you whatever you need."

I heard the front door handle jiggle then the sound of a key being inserted into the lock. Seconds later, Sticks walked in. I turned on the hall light for him. In that brief amount of time, Rad had positioned himself between me and the door. I wasn't sure how decent it looked for us to be standing side by side outside my bedroom.

The three of us stood motionless. Rad spoke first. "Clint, how's that bruise on your cheek?"

I moved to Sticks to take a closer look. "I didn't realize I had hit you in the face. I must have been more aggressive last night than I thought." I hadn't meant for that to sound sexual but did enjoy Rad's shocked look after I said it. I tilted Sticks's head back for better lighting. "Let me get you some ice. It may be too late now though. I didn't notice it this evening."

"I'm alright, Lainee. No need to fuss over it." He took both of my hands in one of his. Then, putting his other arm around me, he turned toward Rad. "Conrad, how are the ribs?"

That's when I figured out the tension wasn't because Rad and I were together in the middle of the night. "You guys did this to each other?"

They kept glaring at one another, ignoring my question.

Rad did answer Sticks eventually. "They're sore, gonna feel them when I move for a while." Then he looked at me. "Glad this happened after our Galveston trip, Lainee."

"That's enough. I told you not to talk about that at the station." Sticks lunged at Rad, knocking a lamp off the hallway console table as they crashed into the wall behind it.

"Stop! That was my grandmother's lamp." The men stood frozen as I knelt to see if anything could be salvaged. "It's ruined."

"Lainee," Sticks said as he touched my shoulder. "You've got to stop putting value in everything your grandmother has touched or said."

A coldness ran through me. My grandmother was the person who always had time for me. She listened to what was going on in my life and gave sage advice. Even death couldn't break the bond with her. Of everyone who had passed through my life, she was the one I missed the most. I removed his hand from my shoulder.

Sticks did not catch on that my silence nor Rad's sharp intake of breath were both hints that he should stop speaking. "You have to learn to move on. This attachment you have is unhealthy."

Tears in my eyes, I walked into my bedroom and closed the door, opening it briefly to give Sticks a pillow and blanket before locking him on the other side.

I could hear Rad's laughter ebb as he walked down the hall. I could only hope his enjoyment hurt his ribs.

Chapter Thirteen
The Cade Zone

I was glad Sticks had already left before I woke up the next morning, if he'd even slept over at all. There was no evidence of the shattered lamp, so I assumed he had stayed long enough to clean it up. After having a good night's sleep, I felt it would be best to make some attempt at forgiving Sticks. After all, he was never witness to any interactions between me and my grandmother and couldn't truly know what she meant to me. In addition, with how his mother had reacted to our marriage and later when he told her he had a daughter, maybe he had never had that kind of a relationship with anyone.

Luckily, I had work to take my mind off the previous night's events. We were studying one of my favorite topics in American History, the original settlements. I loved teaching the students the background in the making of our country. They were producing possible scenarios for what happened to the missing inhabitants of the Roanoke colony, which included everything from alien abduction, conflicts with the Natives, or to being assimilated into a friendly tribe. Their imagination was halted when a maintenance worker walked in and stood directly in front of me.

"I got a request to fix the vents."

"Excuse me, this will have to wait. I have classes until fourth period. After that, I have lunch. You can come back then." I moved around him, directing him toward the door. "In the meantime, you need to check in with the office to get a visitor's pass or have your employee ID visible while in the building."

At this time, three things happened. First, the man grabbed me and pulled me toward the door. Second, Margie, a sweet yet high-spirited student, returned from going to the restroom. She planted her feet and blocked him better than most linebackers could have. Then began yelling for someone to call 9-1-1. He obviously underestimated the strength and voice of a main base cheerleader. And third, some students started banging on the walls to alert others.

Cade was the first teacher on the scene. Margie jumped to the side as he barreled toward us and slammed the man to the floor. She looked as though she might start cheering before quickly running toward the office and yelling for help.

I grabbed my head scarf to bind the man's wrists together. I wasn't sure it would hold, so I reached over and took off Cade's tie, and finished by adding a few knots for reinforcement as an announcement blared overhead for the entire school to go on lockdown.

The school resource officer and assistant principal rushed down the hallway. As the officer led the man away, the AP instructed Cade and me to go to the teacher's lounge. I didn't want to be alone with him, but obligingly followed.

Cade spoke as he closed the door behind us. He put both of his arms around me and held me close. I felt disloyal to Sticks as I returned Cade's hug. God, he felt so solid.

"Lainee, what's going on? Why was that man targeting you? You would have told me if you were in danger, right? I didn't push you that far away, did I?" His voice was gravelly as his hands moved down my back, massaging along their path. I enjoyed his touch until he said, "Let me help."

I pushed away from his embrace. "I'm not a damsel in distress who needs to be rescued by Cade, the Great. You made it clear the night you bailed me out of jail that you are not the person I can turn to."

Cade stepped away, pulling at the cuffs of his sleeves. My guess? He was retreating to the Cade Zone, the place where he shut off all emotions.

Knowing his reactions stemmed from pain and rejection, I slumped into one of the chairs and softened my tone. "I think this has to do with the Bellagio murder. I'm going to have to testify. The authorities"—it seemed callow to bring my husband into the conversation—"think I may be in danger of retaliation."

Cade sat in the chair opposite of me and ran a hand through his blond hair. I noticed he had let it grow out again after having to shave it because of the head injury he received during our summer escapades. I also remembered running my own fingers through it.

"I'm sorry I got you involved. When I hired you to follow Dylan, I never realized how intense it was going to get. Hell, if I'm being honest, I did it to spend more time with you. How pathetic. My solution for being too afraid to ask out the girl I was falling for, was to hire her to investigate my brother."

I needed to process exactly what he was saying and make sure we were on the same thoughtwave. "Was I the only person you hired?"

"Yes, you were."

"So, you were falling for me?"

"What do you want me to say, Lainee? You were the first woman since my broken engagement that I thought I could love?"

My heart was beating faster. I was willing my feet not to act on the urge to go to him and wrap myself around him. Cade was the person merely months before that I thought would be the one for me. Then I remembered how I felt when Rachel had answered the door that morning, with Cade stepping out of his bedroom wrapped in a towel moments later. There was a catch in my breath. It had hurt—still hurt.

Cade looked equally as pained. That was probably how he felt when he walked into the classroom and found out I had gotten married.

And how he felt when he saw Dylan and I on a date.

And when I told him Rad and I were going to Galveston together.

And when he had the suspicion that Sticks had kissed me in the pool house at the party.

And when he said he thought he could love me and I remained speechless.

I was beginning to think the failure of this relationship should be laid directly at my feet.

Cade broke the silence. "Well, it's all come back to bite me in the ass." He laughed ruefully. "I don't know how this could have gone worse for us."

My guilt was eating away at me. I stood and walked around the table, grabbing his hand. I felt the need to explain. "About my marriage, Cade…"

The door opened. The front office secretary came in accompanied by Sticks.

I dropped my hand to my side and leaned against the closest chair for balance. Being in the presence of both men together was unnerving. Cade, with his blond-hair-blue-eyed-cowboy-next-door good looks, and Sticks, with his unpolished handsomeness and dangerous undertones, were silently assessing one another.

And I was assessing my predicament. I had just been caught by my husband holding another man's hand, the morning after being caught outside my bedroom door with yet a different man. Maybe Sticks, who had been trained to pick up on subtle nuances, hadn't noticed. Or possibly he had such keen powers of interpretation that he knew both were innocent situations. I hoped Cade wouldn't antagonize Sticks the way Rad had the previous night. I looked over at Cade. No, he wouldn't. He was staring downward with a look of defeat.

Sticks turned his head to the secretary. "Thanks,

Ms. Kenner. I can manage from here."

"You're welcome. And it's *Miss* Kenner."

I rubbed my forehead and took a calming breath. Caroline Kenner had had her eye on Cade for months and now she was flirting with my husband. Although it was irritating, I couldn't blame her. Sticks's suit must have been custom made to fit his form and he looked rugged with the slight bruising on his left cheek. Cade stood, looking somewhat disheveled with his rumpled hair, missing tie, and top buttons of his shirt undone. He walked to the door, distracting her from Sticks. "Caroline, I'm sure Agent Torres would like to speak to his wife privately."

Her pout of disappointment was quickly replaced by a smile as Cade said, "I'll walk with you to the office. We'll need to discuss how to handle the situation. I'm sure concerned parents will be showing up soon." He held the door open for her as they walked out of the room.

I turned and saw Sticks was watching as I had been fixated on Cade's departure. Sticks leaned on the counter and crossed his ankles while asking, "Is there anything you need to tell me?"

"Is there anything you want to hear?" I countered.

He thought a moment, shook his head slightly, and moved on. "Yesterday evening, we received information of a known accomplice of Mario Bellagio booking a flight to Waco three days from now. The assumption was it would be a threat to you. New intel came in this morning that he was a decoy and the attack was moved up. I only made it to Hillsboro before having to turn around. It's surprising they moved this fast. We need to get you out of their reach." He leaned his head back onto the overhead cabinet. "Damn it. I don't think the FBI will approve the expenses for an around-the-clock guard."

"That's good, because I don't want one."

"I know you don't. Besides, we know how well that went over the last time."

I had no defense. Running away from my security detail was not the best decision I had ever made. Not wanting to admit that aloud, however, I was forced to merely shrug as if it hadn't been a big deal.

"The agency may kill me, but I could take more vacation time. Dean Murphy contacted me. He checked the names from your list and thinks Meredith and Caitlynn might be in New Mexico. We can follow up on that lead together until the trial. That may keep you out of the Bellagio's reach."

So, Dean Murphy was the PI Sticks had hired. Hearing his name out loud irrationally felt like a betrayal. In fact, the whole situation was making me uneasy, so I did what I do best: avoid and redirect. "I can't. I really need the money from subbing and I don't want to leave the school in a bind to get my position covered."

"About that, I was speaking with the principal when this happened. We feel it may be best for your safety," then rushed to add before I could argue, "and for the safety of the students, if you were not in the building until after the trial."

The principal walked into the room. "Oh, Miss

Delaney…"

"Mrs. Delaney-Torres," Sticks corrected, as he winked at me.

"Yes, yes, sorry." The principal continued, "I was needing to find Coach Gainess to see how we could cover your classes for the rest of the day."

I sighed, resigned to my fate, and went to get my things.

Chapter Fourteen
The Shoe Salesman

As we left the building, Sticks said, "I had a unit drop me off so we could ride home together."

"I'm not sure I want to ride with you."

Sticks stopped walking and turned toward me. "Lainee, I apologize for what I said about your grandmother. I was looking at the situation from a clinical perspective, without emotion. It was insensitive for me to make that statement last night."

"Well, that's not all I'm upset about."

"I can't believe you're still mad about Detective Thorpe. Your ex-boyfriend is an ass. His partner stood up and cheered after the fight at the station was over and it wasn't even really a fight. I told him to stop speaking. He got offended and threw a punch. Then I body slammed him to the floor. Is that what this is about?" He sounded incredulous.

"No. But I reserve the right to be mad about that later."

"Is there a statute of limitations here? What is the projected time frame for forgiveness?"

"That type of offense can be drudged up as an example for grandchildren of what not to do. There are other ways to handle matters without resulting in violence." I continued walking and said in a somewhat loud voice, "You could have come to me with the information about the threat. Instead, you go to my boss and ruin any chance I have of working here again."

"It's protocol. When the FBI goes into new territory, we go to the person in charge. We plan out and strategize first." He didn't say it outright, but I got the impression he was implying that I was impulsive.

He continued with his explanation. "Besides, I seem to remember telling you about a threat three months ago and you going off on your own, away from protective custody, resulting in you getting kidnapped, having broken bones, and killing someone."

"This is different, and you are overdramatizing the facts."

"Question, just so I understand. You think I'm the one being overdramatic?"

I ignored him. "One: the threat was to me, not to others. Two: I may have broken two bones, but I only needed one cast. Three: I merely shot someone, not killed them. And four: I did not have complete information. No one told me the whole story then."

In a few strides Sticks was once again beside me. "Lainee, it was an ongoing investigation, no one could tell you the full story. You were told more than enough."

I didn't know if I was angrier at what he had done or at the fact that he was right. "In this case, if you would have come to me with the reasoning of the children's safety, I would have listened. And I could have made an alternate excuse to leave my teaching assignment. Your unwarranted, overprotective display has put my livelihood in danger."

"I'm not going to apologize. The only information we were given was that *something* was going down today." He made air quotation marks as he said the word something. "I did what I did because I was trying to balance my knowledge as an agent and my panic that the nondescript something was going to happen to someone I care about."

He continued talking, but I zoned out when he said he cared about me. He was the third man in less than twenty-four hours to profess feelings for me. Of course, the professions were of varying degrees, but I had no idea what to do. Rad was off limits. The feelings we had were nostalgic and shouldn't be confused as a foundation for the future. I had hurt Cade too much in the short amount of time we were together. Once he started thinking rationally, which would be at any second, he would know I wasn't the right person for him. Plus, I wasn't even sure I should be forgiven for everything I had done to him. Finally, what I had with Sticks was all pretend. What could I consider authentic in our relationship?

I came back on board with the conversation when I noticed he had stopped speaking and was standing with his hands on his hips. He seemed to be expecting a response, so I said the truest words that could be spoken at that time, "I don't know what you expect me to say." I began walking toward my car again.

This made Sticks lose his cool, FBI demeanor. "I am just as new to being married as you are. I don't know what the rules are. Hell, even if I did, I'm sure you would have some convoluted Southern exception to each one. I think it is a spouse's responsibility to protect their partner. That's all I was doing."

Disrespecting my Southern values was going too far. So was his chivalrous protective foolishness. I couldn't have him around me. I needed to get to my car before him. Between my shorter leg span and high heels, that was not going to happen. Taking off one shoe and throwing it at him, unfortunately missing, I began a lopsided dash. "I am so tired of everyone thinking I need to be rescued."

He bent down to retrieve the shoe and started following me, catching up quickly. "What is wrong with people trying to take care of you, Lainee?"

"You better step away. I still have another shoe."

"You didn't answer my question. I'm trying to protect you. Maybe I went overboard, but you have to remember I've been investigating these people for two years. I know what they are capable of, Lainee. Jesus, you know what they're capable of. Don't you remember seeing those men bleeding out while strung up on meat hooks? Do you remember that is what they were planning to do to you?"

I did remember and the fact he was right once again frustrated me even more. I took off my remaining shoe and threw it, this time hitting him, before going at a full out sprint, clicking the key fob. I made it to my car and jumped into the driver's seat, quickly relocking the doors. The look on Sticks's face was worth every ounce of effort as I left him standing in the parking lot.

***

Sticks made it home about an hour later. Hilda and I were in my bedroom. After my parents' deaths, Hilda had been the person I turned to for advice and support. My siblings had abandoned me. Even though we had celebrated the holidays together, almost a year had passed since and my only contact with them afterward had been for our quarterly meetings with the estate accountant. They didn't even know I was married yet.

Sticks hesitated slightly when entering the room, unsure if he was welcome. He wasn't watching me though. His eyes were on Hilda. After seeing her look, I was surprised he hadn't run away screaming. He evidently passed his FBI training on staying calm when being given if-looks-could-kill stares. Hilda was already judge and jury. I had to rescue him before she became executioner, too.

"Sticks and I need to talk privately. Hilda, would you mind?"

"I'll be in the kitchen if you need me." She maintained her evil eye contact with him the entire time she was walking out.

He turned to me, hands on his hips. "You told Hilda? I'm never going to live this down."

After I had come in crying, Hilda drew a bath for

me and set up for a pedicure afterward. My feet were soaking in the foot spa as we enjoyed a glass of sweet tea while talking when Sticks came in. I hadn't intended to tell her, but everything spilled out. And by "everything" in that sentence, I meant I left out the attempted abduction and told her only that Sticks had made a scene at my place of employment.

"You tell my boss. I tell Hilda. Sounds fair to me."

"No, it doesn't. Especially when I came here to tell you I realized my mistake." He opened his briefcase and pulled out my shoes then knelt in front of me. "I can't wait for the opportunity to drudge up shoe throwing as a non-example for grandkids."

"In my defense, I thought with you being an FBI agent and all, you would have had better reflexes and moved out of the way."

He chuckled while drying my feet with a towel and began applying pressure on reflexology points. Then he put one shoe on my foot, kissing along my ankle, repeating the process on the other side. I never knew buckling a shoe could be so sensuous. He grabbed the lotion I had been using for my pedicure and started massaging. He worked magic, first on my calves then moving further up my legs. His mouth followed his hands as he left delicate kisses along their path. I was in nothing but my robe which meant there was nothing impeding his journey. And he was using his all access pass with precision.

Until his phone rang. The ringtone was high-pitched and non-stopping.

"I have to take this." He got up and wiped his

hands and face on the towel before answering. "Torres."

I could only hear his side of the conversation.

"Sir, I understand the timing…Someone from the Dallas or Austin offices can cover…No, I won't change my mind… I have to think about the safety of my wife… The decision is made. I have the time and I'm using it."

Hanging up, he said, "Come on, Lainee. We've got to get away from here. They're sending a car for me."

"Where are we going? What should I pack?" I said to Sticks's back as he walked into my closet.

"New Mexico and anything you think you'll need." He placed my carry-on bag on the bed then began texting as he said, "As long as everything you need fits in this one bag and you can be ready to leave in fifteen minutes. We'll need to be at the airport in an hour."

It was burdensome, but I managed to meet the requirements. I kept my shoes on—not wanting to waste all of Sticks's effort—and added beige capris with a navy and white polka dotted oversized tank tamed at the waist with a yellow belt. I layered the look with a short sleeved white button down top and added a thin-brimmed straw hat with a yellow ribbon band to tame my dark hair that I left flowing down my back.

We were on the main road when we saw a familiar looking black sedan. It kept driving. Yes! We had escaped.

Chapter Fifteen
Mara, the Bitter

Early that evening, I found myself standing in the cul de sac of a trailer park in New Mexico. Even at this hour, my vision was distorted from the waves of heat rising from the pavement. Sticks stood beside me.

The PI he had hired tracked down Meredith to this mobile home community. I couldn't believe Meredith would live here. It showed how desperately she wanted to get away, although I couldn't imagine why she was running from Sticks. We were in an area of depressed economy to say the least. Each trailer was in a various state of disrepair.

We walked to the trailer with a rusted sign I presumed was white with red lettering in its previous life. The corrugated aluminum underpinning was coming away from the base of the porch. I wondered what kind of animals could be scurrying around under there and quickened my steps to get onto the platform.

An older woman came to the doorway smelling of a lifelong love affair with cigarettes.

I asked, "Are you the property manager?"

"Yep, Mara Merriweather." Her eyes looked Sticks up and down as she added, "In the flesh." He didn't take the bait, so she turned toward me and continued, "What're you needing? Don't think you'd be looking for a place here."

I ignored her look of disapproval as I suppressed one of my own. "Actually, we're here to ask about one of your tenants."

"He looks like a cop," she said pointing at Sticks. "So, I'd guess he'd be interested in almost all of my tenants. You, on the other hand, look like ten pounds of bitch in a five-pound bag. I can only think of one person someone like you would be looking for, but you're too late. She and her daughter packed up and moved about two days ago."

"Did she leave a forwarding address?"

"Nope." The manager tried to close the door, but I used my foot as an ineffective doorstop, instantly regretting it. The lady was faster than she appeared. More concerned about damage to my most expensive shoes than a physical injury, I leveraged my weight to free my foot before she could repeat the process.

She didn't. Instead, she moved back, making me fall forward. At least the impact was softened by the dog hair interwoven into the threadbare carpeting that was riddled with little pellets. I was desperately trying to convince myself those droppings were hamster food.

Sticks effortlessly raised me to my feet and said, "Thanks for your help, ma'am. If you hear from her again, please let us know." He held out a card, which she didn't accept. He propped it in the door as we left.

Sticks hurriedly got me into the car.

"Oh, God! Oh, my!" I alternated between using God's name in vain and spitting out dog hair, in addition to rubbing my forearms with my gritty hands from the now crushed pellets that had broken my fall. They seemed to be alive and reproducing at an exponential rate. There was no way I could escape the feeling of being invaded by pathogens.

"Lainee, calm down. Take a deep breath."

I took his advice but wound up sucking in what I hoped was a dog hair and panicked even more.

Sticks was calm. "Stop moving. Breathe through your nose. You're spitting all over yourself and you're actually spreading the feces when rubbing your forearms."

I screeched. "Get me to the hotel. I have to take a shower. Then we need to call the rental company to bring us a new car." Despite his directive, I couldn't stop the repetitive rubbing of my forearms. By that point, I was hoping friction would cause enough heat to kill some of the bacteria. "This is my new outfit, too!" I wiped a tear running down my cheek then cried harder because I had just contaminated my face with the hazardous waste material.

"It's okay, Lainee." Sticks was torn on how to comfort me. He raised his hand above my head like he was going to pat me.

"Don't touch me!"

He gave up and replaced his hand on the steering wheel.

I embraced my pity party. "Look at me. I try for people to take me seriously, and I wind up falling on my face. That lady didn't even want to listen to what I had to say. She thought I was a bitch." I balled my hands into fists and held them in front of me to avoid further defilement. "Everybody has an idea about who I am and what I need. But they can't know, because I don't even know. Cade thinks I need to be rescued all the time. Rad believes I'm a suppressed hedonist. Hilda prays I'll find my way off the path to Hell, but according to Marsha, I'm living the life of a nun. My brother and sister's opinion is that I'm squandering away the family wealth. And who knows what you think of me after all of this." I let the tears flow.

Sticks responded, ticking off statements with his fingers as he went. "I disagree with Cade, you don't need to be rescued, but I'd prefer it if you would stay out of situations that may endanger you in the first place. I haven't seen any of the hedonistic tendencies that Rad mentioned but would be happy to provide the therapy needed to bring those to the forefront. It doesn't hurt to accept as much prayer as you can get, for whatever reason, from Hilda or anyone else. Don't tell her I said this, but Marsha is wrong. I have absolutely no thoughts of you in the nun category. And you can reassure your siblings that on paper, your net worth seems to be intact." Then he placated, "Finally, I think we're at the hotel and can get you all cleaned up so you're feeling better."

I started to reach for the door handle.

"No, no. Let me get that for you, Lainee. Try not to touch anything else."

After helping me out of the car, he led the way through the hotel. When we had checked in, I loved the luxurious lobby with the deep grain mahogany crown moulding accenting the warm hues of the walls and the comforting homestead decor. As I followed him through the lobby the second time, I was acutely aware of the other guests' stares. Sticks pushed the button to the elevator and the doors slid open. I cringed at my image in the mirror on the back wall and saw why I had garnered so much attention. My mascara had left residue congregating below my eyes with some of it escaping in trails down my cheeks. I was holding my forearms up and in front of me with my fists balled as if I were defending off an unseen attacker.

We made it to our hotel room with Sticks unlocking and opening all doors along the way and finally depositing me in the bathroom after turning on the water for a hot shower.

I stepped under the stream of water, fully clothed. Sticks unwrapped the bar of soap and gave it to me. "I'll let you have some privacy," he said, quietly closing the door behind him.

I began vigorously rubbing my forearms and hands with the soap, debating on whether to wash my mouth out with it. Convinced I had disinfected everything, I took off my clothes and let them drop to the floor of the tub.

Once I finished showering, I went to the sink. Antiseptic mouthwash became my best friend and brushing my teeth became a cardio exercise. I heard a faint knocking at the door and Sticks opened it only wide enough to place my bag on the floor.

"Why don't you get dressed and we'll go to dinner? It may help take your mind off today's events."

I did one last glance in the mirror. The yellow sundress I had chosen dipped low in front but maintained modesty by camouflaging my cleavage with a ruffled neckline. I ran a brush through my hair and was doing the final touch up for my mascara when the room phone rang. I could hear the deep timbre of Sticks's voice as he answered.

When I emerged from the bathroom, Sticks said, "I have great news."

"That's what I need. Let me hear it." I sank into the armchair opposite of him.

"Someone called with information about Meredith. They got my number from Mara and want to meet tomorrow."

"I'm not going back to that trailer park." Suddenly feeling grimy, I fought the urge to take another shower.

"Don't worry, Lainee, we're going to meet here."

I took some deep breaths and calmed.

"I have even better news," Sticks continued, "The car company sent a new rental, so we won't have to eat here at the hotel." He was searching through the welcome materials on the table. "I thought you might enjoy going here. I know you dressed up as a flapper when you were in college. The atmosphere combines a prohibition era hideaway theme with a five-star menu." He gave me a brochure. "You need a reservation and a password to get in, but the hotel has a standing reservation for a limited number of guests. The front desk clerk gave me the password if you'd like to go. Are you up for steak or lobster?"

"Sounds wonderful." I pointed to the brochure. "It says here that '20s-style dress is encouraged." I grabbed my shoes from the doorway and moved to the bed and put them on, wishing Sticks would offer a repeat of his afternoon performance. "If I'd have known, I would have brought my fringe dress. We could pretend we're undercover, going there for a raid. This is the perfect setting for an FBI agent and a private investigator to go on their first date."

"Kind of odd phrasing since we're married."

"Yes, there is that little technicality."

Chapter Sixteen
The Speakeasy

Dinner was a unique dining experience. At first, we couldn't find the restaurant, so we took a shot and went into Vincent's Grocery. Once inside the cramped store, you had to find the secret entrance. Toward the rear, there was a large black door with an illuminated red light above it. We knocked and were admitted after Sticks told the man behind it our password. After being ushered through plush, red velvet drapes into a dark room, we sat in overstuffed chairs across from the bar until our table was ready.

It was like being transported to a different age. The décor was designed of crates showcasing '20s memorabilia. Our table was candle-lit, and entertainment was provided by a live band playing in the adjacent lounge. The meal was expertly prepared and presented. I stuck with a light appetizer of asparagus con carne and a watercress salad. Sticks went with a classic filet mignon and added lobster tail.

Toward the end of dinner, Sticks said, "I checked my email while you were showering. There was a message from my lawyer. I had told him to go ahead and draw up papers so we could file them quickly once Meredith was found." He motioned for the waiter. "He said there was a complication about our marriage.

Do you know what that could be about?"

"Well, there are several things: everything being a sham, your mother hating me, all the lies we have to tell. I could go on." I fidgeted with the butter knife left in the bread basket. "Our marriage is causing me a lot of stress. I feel like I'm teetering on the edge of a cliff."

"I didn't realize we were having that many issues. I was thinking our only problem was that we haven't had sex yet."

I laughed.

"Hon, I wasn't joking. I had no idea you were that unhappy, but I'm glad we're talking about this now. What's your major concern?"

The waiter brought our tab and quietly left.

"The lies. I'm hurting so many people. Everyone around me thinks I'm impulsive and making bad decisions. They're worried this is a reaction to my parents' deaths." It was almost two years, but my emotions were still so raw it felt like yesterday. "Kyle cornered me in the teacher's lounge and asked me if I was suffering from Stockholm Syndrome and accused me of falling in love with my hero."

Kyle was Cade's best friend. We all worked together at the school. I omitted the fact that Kyle also stated if that were the case, I had fallen in love with the wrong hero. He made the argument that sometimes heroes were the ones you could rely on day in and out.

"You don't have to worry about Stockholm Syndrome. That's falling in love with your captor. The term here is White Knight Syndrome. As for me being a hero, you should hear my mother's version of how we met. That part of the rumor might be her fault."

"Well, she's another obstacle. Everybody loves me when they meet me. Your mom hated me."

"She didn't hate you." In response to my raised eyebrow, he added, "She didn't approve of the situation. Slowly but surely, she'll come around." He checked the tab, added a generous tip, then signed the bill. "And you may want to reevaluate your 'everybody loves me' statement. I've heard about a few of your interactions with Roxanne. Then there's the kidnapping situations—notice that word was with an 's'—two months ago, along with you being held at gunpoint last month, as well as the attempted abduction this morning."

He said it jokingly, but it made me realize the biggest problem with our marriage and getting custody of Caitlynn.

"I think the lawyer was referring to me. I'm the complication. It doesn't matter that you're traveling all the time and I have the consistent residence with a stable background. After these last few months, no court is going to allow a child into that much danger. I'm not helping you at all. This ruse was for nothing."

He reached out and held my hand. "I'm sure that's not what he meant. I don't want you to get upset. Let's table this conversation for now and enjoy the rest of our evening together. All we're doing is speculating. We can't fix any of these issues tonight. I'll see what I can find out tomorrow."

***

We were silent on the drive. Sticks was casually holding my hand, intermittently caressing it with his thumb. I was amazed at how he could be so solid and rough, yet caring and gentle.

I stared out the window, looking at the city lights passing as we made our way to the hotel, trying to keep my mind off the thought of how Sticks looked lounging in only his underwear on my bed the other week or how his mouth felt on my body earlier that day. Sticks reached to adjust the radio and moved his hand to my thigh. The anticipation of what would happen once we got to our destination was growing each second.

As he exited the interstate onto the access road and came to a stop at a red light, I kept hearing Marsha's voice in my head. It was telling me about the advantages of having sex on a first date. However, I had made the decision that the hotel was not going to be where the big event occurred. If I was going to have sex on a first date, it was going to be impulsive and uncontrolled.

"There is one problem with our marriage we could fix tonight, Sticks. Maybe we should think about your major concern." I tugged his shirt from his pants and began unbuttoning.

His breath became heavier as he replied, "Yes, that one could be solved fairly quickly."

"Hopefully, not too quickly, Sticks," I said as I

leaned over to kiss him.

"I'm not making any guarantees." Then whispered, "The first time."

I enjoyed the lingering kiss along with Sticks's well-orchestrated hand motions until the car behind us honked.

Sticks pulled through the light and into a shopping center, parking behind the secluded building. He turned off the car. "Lainee, are you sure you want to do this now?"

"I'm more than ready," I said as I crawled over the console, straddled him, and unzipped his pants to begin actively pursuing my goal.

He pushed a button and the seat reclined. I shifted to allow him to lift my dress over my hips. Once that was done, simply sliding aside my panties was all it took to remove every barrier.

***

"That was worth getting a misdemeanor, possibly felony, depending on what part we were caught doing." Sticks stroked my hair while I contentedly nestled into his chest.

After a while, he said, "Lainee, it's getting late. Let's get back to the hotel."

I raised onto my elbows. "Was pointing out the time your subtle way of patting yourself on the back for how long you lasted?"

"That's me wanting to hurry so we can do it again." He boosted me up and over the console then arranged himself by simply tucking it to the left so it would fit under the waistband of his boxers. He zipped his pants, leaving his shirt open, exposing his broad chest. As he started the car, he said, "For the record, my back is not what I want patted."

The afterglow was beginning to wear off as we had come full circle, waiting at another traffic light. I began worrying about the lack of a particular type of barrier.

"Sticks, we left out a very important element in our activity back there."

"We left out quite a bit, hon. I promise we'll get around to it when we take our time at the hotel."

"That's not what I was referring to. You didn't happen to have a vasectomy in the last 15 years, did you?"

"I saw the pill in your luggage. I assumed you had that covered."

Before I could respond, we were thrown forward. My shoulder hit the dash and the seat belt caught my neck in its grip. I looked behind us and saw we had been rear-ended.

"Are you okay, Lainee?"

"I'm fine. How about you?"

"Physically fine. Disappointed about the timing." He buttoned his shirt askew and hastily tucked it in his pants. "We're definitely going to have to discuss this later. You'd think I'd have learned my lesson about sex in cars." He draped his jacket around me. "You look like you've been doing exactly what we've been doing. You may want to stay in the car." He gave me a quick peck as he got out.

Chapter Seventeen
The Backdoor Trojan

Something was off. Three men had gotten out of their car and surrounded Sticks. I took Sticks's gun from the pocket of his jacket. I wasn't a member of the good ol' boy gun club and I wasn't sure exactly what I needed to do to shoot this gun. I had only practiced with my grandfather's old service revolver or my newly acquired dainty and pink .38 Smith and Wesson. I had never shot a handgun without first cocking the hammer, although I knew it could be done on mine. I simply didn't like having to use more force to pull the trigger. This gun didn't have an exposed hammer. I didn't even know if it had a safety, much less how to disengage it if needed. Maybe just the threat of the gun would be enough for the men to get back in their car and allow Sticks and I to leave.

Not wanting to tip off the men, I took the keys from the ignition to disengage the clanging alert bell then felt the roof of the car for the dome light and made sure it was turned off. Quietly opening the door and sliding out, I ducked as I walked to the rear of the car. I stood up and raised the gun, distracting the men while Sticks tackled one of them. The two left standing were not concerned that I had a firearm. One pulled out his own and did not hesitate to shoot. I crouched behind the car. The bullet pinged off the trunk to the right of my head. The one on the ground recovered quickly and, with the assistance of the third man, grabbed Sticks and shuffled him into the backseat. The shooter climbed into the driver's seat, while the other two jumped into the back.

I needed to gather as much information as possible. I made mental notes on the car description, which wouldn't help, considering all I knew was that it was a dark color, had tinted windows, and was a four-door sedan. There were no visible make and model emblems, and I couldn't read the license plate as it sped away.

I hurriedly got into our rental, having to now turn on the dome lights and search for the keys, while also digging through my purse to get my phone. I started the car, put it in gear and ran the red light, thankful there was no traffic. I found my phone. The first person I dialed? Dylan. I had no clue what cases Sticks was working on and wasn't sure if calling the police would jeopardize him more or help him.

"Gainess," he answered.

"Dylan, they took Sticks. They shot at me. Were they FBI? They were sending a car for him when we left. Should I contact the police? I don't know what he's involved in."

"God, Lainee. He's involved with you. What the hell happened?" He let out a big breath. "No, don't tell me. Tell the police. It's not the FBI. I'll notify people on my end." He hung up.

I hurriedly punched the numbers.

"9-1-1. What's your emergency?"

"My husband has been taken. They hit us then took him."

"Ma'am, remain calm. Are you injured?"

"No."

"Okay. Where are you?"

I took a deep breath. Answering questions was not the form of action I needed to be taking. "Not sure. We're from out of town. The nearest highway sign says Carlisle Boulevard half mile and San Mateo Boulevard three-quarters of a mile."

I could hear him typing in the background. "A unit has been dispatched. That means you are facing west."

"No. It means I'm driving west."

"So, you're in a car? Your car was hit, not you personally?"

"Correct. My husband got out to check the damage and exchange information. He's an FBI agent."

"Was his abduction a part of a case? Who's his agent in charge? What's your husband's name?"

I was desperately trying to keep the car in my sights. It was moving at a high rate of speed. "I don't know if this is related. He's the supervisory special agent in charge of the Bellagio case. His name is Clint Torres."

The operator paused. "And your name?"

"Lainee Delaney."

A longer pause. "Ma'am, it is an offense to prank

the emergency line. I have dispatched a unit just in case, but people shouldn't waste our time when we can be helping others." He ended the call.

I dialed a third time. "Lucas?"

"Miss Delaney." His monotone voice boomed through the phone as I placed it away from my ear.

Lucas was a former student of mine from substituting. There was a slight misunderstanding about his internship, along with him trespassing and breaking and entering on my property during my previous case. He had an interest in private investigating, made borderline obsession by his autism.

"I'm actually Mrs. Torres." Saying Delaney-Torres didn't seem nearly as important. I needed that connection to Sticks, even if it was in name only.

"I can't talk to strangers."

Third call. Third hang up.

I redialed his number. "Lucas, don't hang up. It's Miss Delaney but I got married and changed my name. I need your help."

"Is this for a case? Will I be a consultant again? I may want to renegotiate my salary. My dad is keeping a closer eye on my online purchases. I don't know what that means though because his eyes don't look that much closer to me."

His interpretation of life was uplifting, but I had to get him to assist me. "Can you track my husband's cell phone like you did Ashley's this summer?"

"Yes. Tell me the digits. I'll see if there's a backdoor Trojan to get in." I rattled off the number and barely had time to ponder what backdoor Trojan may mean before he said, "Got it. He's moving west on Interstate 40."

I saw flashing red and blue lights in the mirror and pulled to the side.

"You're in luck. The car is slowing."

I came to a complete stop as the officer made short bursts of the siren.

"Now, it's stopped. That's strange. It didn't exit or anything. It's just stopped on the road."

"Lucas, do me a favor. Can you call the number?" I felt a vibration in the jacket pocket.

Chapter Eighteen
The Waiting Place

That began my night in the waiting place and I don't do well waiting. I decided to call Marsha and give her an update before being called in for the interrogation.

She answered immediately. "Lainee, what is going on? Are you okay?"

I sighed. "I guess you spoke with Dylan."

"Spoke with him? No. It is more like I overheard your conversation. To say the least, your call definitely changed the mood of our evening. And you still haven't answered my questions."

"Yes, I'm fine, but I'm not sure about Sticks, and I can tell that even though I'm his wife, neither the police department nor the FBI is going to give me many updates." Their lack of communication may have been fair, since I wasn't giving them the full story either. No one needed to know the reason Sticks and I had gotten married. "I'm going to have to look into this myself."

"No. No, you don't have to do that."

"Yes, I do. I owe it to Sticks to do everything in my power to find him."

"Is there anything I can say to change your

mind?"

"No."

Marsha responded, "Then I'll revise my earlier statement. You don't have to do that alone. I'll text you my flight details. Just make sure you pick me up from the airport."

I could feel the tension release in my shoulders. I hadn't known I was so tense. "Thanks, Marsha."

***

During the interrogation, I told the police about my almost abduction that morning, they considered me a vulnerable witness and wanted my statement video recorded. I had already written it and was waiting for the FBI to question me to see if I needed to add more details before recording.

I spent most of that time thinking about Sticks. When we first met, I saw nothing but his gruff exterior. Of all the men repelling from the helicopter to the rescue that day, Sticks was the one that stood out. Dangerous and powerful were my initial impressions. Somewhere along the way, probably in Arizona, he became softer. Seeing him with his mother provided a new perspective. A perspective that was not sharing the limelight. Our marriage may not have been founded on love, but there was mutual respect, and I didn't want it to end because of the death-do-us-part clause. *How do you want it to end?* The question flashed through my mind and I chose to ignore it.

Morning was breaking as I made it to the hotel room. Entering alone was not the plan I had had the previous evening. I flipped on the light, startled to see someone sitting in one of the armchairs. Even more startled to see he was my seatmate from the flight back from Arizona.

The FBI had taken Sticks's gun and mine was still in Texas along with my pepper spray. The realization I had no weapon did not deter me from digging through my handbag. The closest thing I found to a weapon was my lavender scented hand sanitizer.

"Lainee, it's good to see you again," he said smiling.

"How do you know my name?" I mentally thumped my forehead. A man that I met briefly during a flight had tracked me down and was sitting in my hotel room. There were many more unanswered questions than how he knew my name.

His thick gold chain necklace stood out against his black mock turtleneck paired with gray sheen dress pants. His dark hair, silvered at the temple, was worn slicked back and held in place by more hair products than I used in a month.

"I am Ronaldo Bellagio."

Bellagio. I didn't wait any longer. I opened the door and ran.

Not far though. I immediately hit the back of one of the two beefy men blocking the doorway. He quickly turned, picked me up, and deposited me on the couch.

"There's no need for theatrics." One of the goons

coughed at Ronaldo's statement. "I abandoned my uncle's code long ago. I do, however, still keep in touch with my cousin, Marguerite. She sends her appreciation for the role you played in her father's demise."

Ronaldo had been stone-faced throughout the conversation. His companion's reaction earlier though had me concerned about their plans.

He got up and walked over to me. "Piccolo, calm yourself." His statement meant, despite my wish otherwise, he had seen the panicked rise and fall of my chest as my breath quickened and heard the slight squeal I emitted after being man-handled by his henchman.

Ronaldo reached toward my face. I was not going to flinch. I had been in much worse situations. No one here was brandishing a weapon. I wasn't enclosed in a dark, small area, and I was only outnumbered three to one. Okay, that last one was bad.

He touched my earring, stroking it, then said, "Lovely." He then stroked his thumb over my cheek and said, "Lovelier."

I scanned the room for anything to use as a weapon. The balcony wouldn't be a good route. Even if I could possibly jump off then swing onto the one beneath, I didn't think the laws of probability were in my favor. There was the glass coffee table. Maybe I could break it and brandish a sliver of glass to make them back away while I left. Except they could also get a broken piece. If I were lucky, that would result in a standoff. And considering the three to one ratio, the odds were once again not in my favor. My only way out of this, or at least to buy more time, would be to start talking. I asked with bravado, "What did you do to my husband?"

"We did nothing to him. His abduction is why I had to make my presence known." Ronaldo returned to his seat and placed one ankle on his other knee. "I was sent by Marguerite to protect you."

"So, she really is thankful that I shot her father? I thought that was a veiled threat."

"When I threaten people, there is no shroud. Marguerite planned to overtake the family business and legalize it for years. After Uncle Mario killed her son, she no longer wanted to wait, but your actions benefitted her scheme. Her father was out of the way and no suspicions were cast upon her."

"Her son? In all the research I've done," which amounted to one episode of my true crime shows, "a son was never mentioned."

"He's mentioned all the time but erroneously reported as her brother. You knew him as Paulo." He took a sip of the drink he had been holding and motioned for one of the men to make another.

"That's an interesting story, but I need to focus on Sticks. If you didn't take him, who did? And why didn't you stop them?"

"Little One, you misunderstood. I'm here to make sure nothing bad happens to you. The FBI agent you call husband is none of my concern."

"If you're here to protect me, then you're going to have to follow me. I'm rescuing Sticks." I began walking toward the door.

"Wait, wait, wait." Ronaldo's demeanor fell apart. "I'm really a theatre director and these are two of my actors. People haven't appreciated the arts in my hometown as much as I had anticipated. I had to go to my cousin for a loan, but she said I would have to earn it. She gave me a credit card and five thousand dollars to keep an eye on you."

The goons, still in character stood shoulder to shoulder. The only break in protocol was when one leaned to the other and said, "Five thousand? He's seriously underpaying us."

I stepped again toward the exit. Ronaldo got up and stood between me and the door. "Please don't make me call Marguerite and tell her I've lost you. They're already on their way." He interlaced his fingers as if he were praying. "Please. Don't leave."

"If Marguerite's going legal, why are you so scared of her?"

"I should clarify and say she's moving in a more legalized fashion. She still has to walk the fine line keeping up with appearances."

I readjusted my bag on my shoulder. "I'm not staying, but you can ride with me to the airport. My friend is on her way to help me out."

One of the men spoke. "Calling your cousin for backup is getting us in too deep. If you don't mind, could you pay us now and we'll be on our way?"

Ronaldo pulled out some cash and gave each man two one-hundred-dollar bills.

This time the second man spoke. "I want to

change our agreement. Five bills each seems fair now that we know what we got ourselves into."

Ronaldo sighed and peeled off six more and handed them to the men. "Okay, but you'll need to find your own way home," he said as he stuffed the remainder in his jeans pocket.

Normally, my Southern belle manners told me to be patient. However, there was another facet overtaking those sensibilities. I had visions of me in pink camouflage double fisting AK-47s, hosing down anyone who got in the way of me rescuing Sticks. I suppressed the automatic weapons vision and simply walked out the door in the middle of their conversation.

Ronaldo caught up to me at the elevator.

Chapter Nineteen
True South

As we stepped into the elevator, I couldn't resist asking, "How were you planning on protecting me? I mean, I was almost abducted from my job and my husband was kidnapped from right under your nose. You don't seem to be well-suited for the task."

"I might not have experience, but I'm very resourceful." He pushed the button for the ground floor. "Did you notice there was no getaway car at the school? I took care of that by doing a hit and run on the van. When the school officer came out to investigate, the driver took off. The man who tried to grab you wouldn't have had anywhere to go."

"All that means is there's a man lurking somewhere who could come back for me at any minute."

"Well, I didn't think of it that way. In my mind, I was more or less expecting a thank you."

The doors to the elevator opened into the hotel lobby. We walked through the maze of guests leaving or heading to the breakfast area. My stomach was queasy from hunger and my head ached from lack of sleep, but I needed to keep going.

Once we got outside and made it into the car, I continued my questioning. "Why didn't you intervene when they took Sticks? The threat wasn't to me, but you couldn't have known that."

"To be honest, we weren't watching you at the time. I figured you'd be safe with an FBI agent, so we took a break. After three hours, we got curious and found out you were at the police station."

I pulled into traffic and began making my way toward the interstate. "How did you know I was there?"

Ronaldo looked sheepish as he admitted, "I planted a tracking device on you on the plane. I'm glad you hadn't changed purses."

"If I wasn't driving, I would find it and get rid of it. The first chance I get, I will. Don't think that trick will work again."

He held both palms up in surrender, "I won't."

We drove along I-25 and took the exit to Albuquerque International Sunport. As we approached the arrivals area, Marsha texted that she had gotten her luggage and was waiting.

I saw her standing with a porter. He was taking her full set of luggage off the cart. I silently gave praise for Marsha's ability to pack hurriedly and without thought to what she actually needed. I was sure she brought everything I couldn't with my one bag limitation.

I pulled to the curb beside her. She looked sexy chic in her terracotta undershirt with a flowing sheer cardigan, paired with brown mini shorts and matching brown strappy sandals that accented her long, athletic legs. Her long, blond hair was pulled into a ponytail.

Marsha gave me a questioning look, obviously wondering who was with me. I popped open the trunk and the porter began loading. She pulled out a twenty, handed it to him, opened the front passenger door, and stood waiting.

I leaned to Ronaldo. "She's waiting for you to be a gentleman and sit in the back."

"You're kidding, right?"

I shrugged. He reluctantly moved.

Marsha was snooty. "Who are you?"

"I'm Ronaldo. I'm helping keep an eye on Lainee."

Marsha looked at me for confirmation.

I pulled into the airport traffic. "He's a Bellagio but was sent to make sure I'm safe."

Marsha began digging through her purse. "Damnit, next time we take a case away from home, we're driving. I got nothing. Airport security even took my nail files. I don't like not having a gun."

"I had one, but the FBI confiscated it."

"Another example of the government restricting our Second Amendment rights."

"Marsha, it was their property. It was the one issued to Sticks."

"Well, I guess that's okay then." She flipped down the visor and checked her lipstick. "Tell me what's going on. Has anything changed since we talked?"

"Only having the tag along has changed." I merged onto the freeway. "Did Dylan give any indication of who he thought might be responsible?"

Marsha looked toward the man sitting quietly in the backseat. "Are you sure we can trust him? They're working under the theory it's the Bellagios taking Sticks to control your testimony."

"He's not active in the family business. Right now, he's an unemployed actor trying to scrape some money together."

Ronaldo finally spoke, "Hey, I am employed right now. I thought I was convincing as a mob boss."

Marsha ignored him. "They are keeping an open mind to other possibilities. Dylan said Sticks wanted to take time off for personal reasons. Does that have anything to do with why you got married?"

"Maybe he wanted the time off *because* we got married." Marsha didn't look convinced, so I continued, "You know, to take little trips with his new wife, like this one."

"I might have believed that if you hadn't come to Albuquerque."

Changing the subject, I said, "I think we should concentrate on how his abductors knew where we would be."

"How did this one track you down?"

"This one, as you call him, is the man I told you about from my flight. He put a locating device in my purse then. That reminds me," I handed my bag to Marsha. "Can you find it in here and throw it out, please?"

Ronaldo spoke again, "Don't throw it out. I can disable it. Those things are expensive. I can pawn it when all of this is over."

"Throw it out." I repeated.

I was startled minutes later by Marsha rolling down the window.

"Don't be so jumpy," Ronaldo huffed from the backseat. "She just found it and got rid of it like you asked."

"Are you okay, Lainee?" Marsha seemed concerned.

"It must be my lack of sleep. Let's get to the hotel. I'll take a nap while you unpack. I'm sure Ronaldo will help you carry in your luggage."

"Sure, assume because I'm male, I'll do the heavy lifting. One more reason to avoid Texans."

Marsha turned in her seat. "It has nothing to do with you being male. We assume people will be polite in the South. Where are you from anyway?"

"Nebraska."

She turned toward me. "A northerner and a Bellagio. Why are we trusting him?"

Ronaldo was indignant. "Northerner? Do they even teach geography in Texas? Nebraska is the Midwest."

"If you're from north of Texas, you're a Northerner. Texas is the only true southern state. If it weren't for OU, I'd accept Oklahoma."

"What about all of the other states that are considered southern? Have you ever heard of Mississippi, Alabama, Georgia?"

"Those others are easterners and being from the South is on their wishlist."

I had never seen Marsha so adamant about Texas. She usually chided me when I got on my Southern exceptionalism kick. However, my head was aching too much to intervene.

I pulled into the parking space, "Marsha, come up with me, then I'll give you the key to get all your things squared away."

I took a much-needed shower after the previous night's activity and barely made it to the bed before falling asleep.

Chapter Twenty
With the FBI

I awoke with a plan. "Marsha," I yelled as I jumped out of bed and headed to the bathroom.

She stuck her head through the door.

"I think you were right. It may be something related to his personal time off." Throughout our investigation, I couldn't imagine a reason Meredith would run from Sticks. So, if she wasn't running from him, who was she running from? "We need to see a woman named Mara. How are we going to get past Ronaldo?"

"He left. Said he had to get ready for his cousin's arrival."

It seemed too suspicious to be true, but I couldn't worry about it. I needed to prepare for Mara. This time, I wore a simple t-shirt, jeans, and running shoes. I glanced at Marsha. She had on the same outfit from the airport, but we didn't have time for her to dress down.

For the second time in two days, I found myself in the cul de sac of the trailer park on the outskirts of Albuquerque.

Only this time, there was yellow crime scene tape

around Mara's porch. A scraggly-haired man who was missing a front tooth approached us. "You needin' help?" He held out his hand. "Wes Phillips. Maintenance."

I shook it, wishing I'd encountered his friendliness the day before. "Lainee Delaney." Then quickly added, "Torres."

"If you're looking, we only got the one place down there." He gestured toward the end of the drive, then pointed to the manager's mobile home. "I think I'm going to salvage this one. No one would want to live there now, not after Mara got killed." His voice cracked as he hung his head low and pinched the bridge of his nose. "Excuse me, she was a wonderful woman."

"My husband and I met her yesterday. I'm sorry for your loss."

"Oh, you must be the lady that went and fell. She was worried 'bout you."

I was wondering if we were speaking of the same woman.

Wes continued, "This means you'll find out who did this, you being with the FBI and all."

"Yes." I didn't contradict his statement because what he said was true. I was *with* the FBI when I met Mara, not a *part* of it. Since my father and brother were lawyers, I learned very early that wording and timing were much more important than meaning. "Would you mind answering a few questions?"

Marsha, usually up for anything, gave me a wary look. It was obvious her free spirit was balking at impersonating a federal agent.

"I'll do anything to help you find whoever did this to my sweet Mara." That was an ironic sentence considering Mara meant bitter in Hebrew.

"Let's go to my house. Would you like a glass of tea?"

We followed Wes into his trailer, which appeared to be one of the newer ones in the community. It was cramped but clean. We chose to sit on the couch, whereas he sat in one of the swivel chairs in front of a sparkling clean front window. It was much different than the filth we encountered the previous day at Mara's.

"I can't believe this happened. We were sitting here last night talkin' 'bout her fine guests. Said she needed to get 'em out before all of the renters up and moved. No offense, but most people here don't want the law in their business." He stared at the empty swivel next to him, probably imagining her there. "She told me you were looking for Jessie and Noemi. Those two were a pair. Came in looking ragged, but after a while you could tell they didn't belong here. Only trouble we had from them was when Mara told her she didn't pull up anything on the background check. That's so unusual, most people here have several tags from their past. It got Mara suspicious. Said she was gonna follow up. Thought it might have been a child custody case or something." Wes chuckled. "That's the only time I saw Jess have that redheaded temper. Next morning, she was gone."

Redhead with the nickname of Meredith's best

friend and the Spanish version of her other best friend's name for the daughter. I was positive this was Meredith and Caitlynn.

Wes had an epiphany. "Say, you don't think Jess had anything to do with it?"

"It could be related. We haven't formed a theory. Investigation's still in the early stages." I was noncommittal, not wanting to lead or alter his line of reasoning.

"I thought it might have somethin' to do with Mara enforcin' the rules. Maybe one of the renters got mad. It's a rough crowd here." He buried his face in his hands. "I found her. Tied to that chair. Cut marks. Slices everywhere. Who could do that to her?"

Flashes of seeing Bellagio's henchmen hung upside down, eviscerated, intestines protruding from their abdomen, and blood covering their faces, dripping from the slits in their throats came to mind, making me jump as I fought the urge to escape. Thankfully, if one could be thankful in that situation, Wes was still reliving his own nightmare and didn't notice.

Marsha furrowed her brow. A look that clearly, yet silently, asked, *"What the hell?"*

I covered by walking over to Wes and touched his forearms, gently guiding them to his lap. I sat in the chair beside him. "I've seen horrors in my investigations as well. I never wish those images for anyone else. I'm sorry this happened to you."

He nodded his head, acknowledging my words. "I got a box of Jessie's things. Had to clean out the trailer after she left. Thought she'd be back for it. They didn't have much to begin with. Think it'd help?"

Marsha chimed in, "Couldn't hurt." She darted her eyes to his front window. A police unit was driving through the property entrance.

Wes rose from his chair and walked down a narrow-paneled hallway, returning minutes later with a half-filled black trash bag.

Marsha and I stood. Both of us understanding we needed to leave as soon as possible before the police could blow our cover. She reached for the bag while I shook his hand. "Thanks for the evidence. We will let you know if we need more information."

Chapter Twenty-One
Trashed Treasure

Marsha and I returned to the hotel room. As soon as I closed the door Marsha asked, "What were you thinking? Dylan is an agent. Sticks is an agent. We," she gestured back and forth between us, "are not! There is a federal law against what we just did."

I raised the bag. "But look what we got from it. It could help us find Sticks."

"Do you know what would help us find Sticks? The police and the FBI."

"Where is your sense of adventure? You're always the 'I'm down for anything friend' and I'm the one who is afraid to take baby steps."

"My sense of adventure is in the hospital room where I left it." She sat on the couch. "I'm thinking before I make decisions now. For the most part, anyway." She began crying. "I made a few today that I'm starting to regret."

I sat beside her and put my arm around her. "What happened?"

"Dylan and I broke up. If you could call it that. We never were official."

"Oh, no!"

"He told me he refused to let me come to New

Mexico. Said the last time I helped you out, he almost lost me after he had just found me." Marsha sniffed. "You know that my system automatically rejects chivalrous twaddle."

"It sounded more like romantic drivel to me." At least that comment made her smile. "I'm sad for you. I thought Dylan might have been your happily ever after."

"You know I'm the multiple happy endings kind of girl, Lainee." Marsha crumpled into a ball and sobbed into the decorative couch cushion.

"Aww, honey." I began rubbing her back. "I'm so sorry."

She sat upright, almost knocking me off the couch. "You should be. Why do you keep putting yourself in danger where other people feel obligated to protect you? Then you pull your exasperated belle routine and tell everyone you can take care of yourself."

I remained calm. Marsha and I had been friends since middle school. I had never seen her act this way. I had also never seen her in a hospital, fighting for her life until last month. I knew the two had to be related. Her comments were coming out of fear not out of anger. I needed to keep reminding myself of that fact.

What I wanted to say was, *"Go diddle yourself. I got out of both of my kidnappings and helped another person escape from her abductor, all without anyone's help."* That statement was true unless you factored in the following: One, Sticks's team in the woods, who were called in to rescue Cade, not me. Two, the paramedics at the meat processing plant, who were called to treat Marcus, not me. Or three, a perfectly timed verbal intervention from the Hamilton County Sheriff's department, who were called to rescue Ashley, not me. The pattern clearly shows none of those three elements should count against my ability to handle myself in dangerous situations.

Instead of any of those comments, I simply stated, "I'm scared, too, Marsha."

That time, she embraced me. When she had cried herself out, she stood and walked over to the trash bag we got from Wes. "Let's see what we got in here."

Most of the items could be considered trash, but Marsha and I both homed in on one item in particular. It was a floral cardboard file box. She got to it before I could and took off the lid.

Inside, there were small scraps of paper, a few business cards, and some larger folded sheets. The scraps of paper included math computations.

Marsha put the calculations aside, but one of them caught my attention. There were three two-digit numbers added together next to another column of three two-digit numbers.

"Marsha, stop a second. These look like birthdays." One was the date of the prom when Caitlynn was conceived. The other date was almost nine months later, probably Caitlynn's actual birthday. "And look at these," I said as I pointed to the other scraps. "There are three, two, then four-digit numbers subtracted from one another, but the final answer is incorrect. They might be social security numbers." I bet if I ran this information through my software, all would be related to Meredith and Caitlynn.

I gathered the business cards next and read them aloud. "Bill Scott, a lawyer in Arizona with the firm Scott, Bennett, and Foreman." Meredith's married name was Bennett. I flipped to the next card. "CareRight Home Healthcare for the Elderly. It's generic. No name, only the business phone and address are listed." I read in the yearbook that Meredith's plan after graduation was to become a nurse like her mother. If I called, I was sure her mother would be an employee there.

Both Marsha and I looked at one another as I flipped to the third and last card which had the FBI emblem emblazoned on the left side. On the bottom right, the name Clint Torres.

Marsha stood then grabbed the card. "Lainee, this is it. You have to tell me what's going on. Right now." She jabbed the card in the air to emphasize her statement.

"Okay. I don't think it will be a breach of Clint's trust since you're here to help." I took the box to the couch, sat down, and filled her in.

After I had finished, Marsha asked, "So you think these may be clues to her true identity in case something happened to her?"

"Yes," I answered. "And I think the people she's running from are the same people who have Clint. Meredith didn't run because Sticks found out about Caitlynn."

"I knew there had to be a reason for you to get married. It wasn't adding up at all." She walked over to the minibar. "I need a drink. Do you want one?"

"I can't this early in the day, Marsha."

She smiled. "I'm doing something reckless and you're being on the straight and narrow." She took a straight shot of bourbon. "Everything is getting back to normal."

"I need to be alert. Everything in this box has been important. Let's see what else we have here." I pulled out the folded sheets of paper. Their significance wasn't as obvious to me. All four sheets contained printed maps of trails. There were red or green triangles in the middle of each. One was labeled Lincoln Tract Campground, another Mooreland Campground, with the other two pages being zoomed-in versions of those sites.

I took out my cell phone and did an Internet search. Both were off Highway 63 around Tererro, New Mexico, which was north of Pecos, all in all about a one-and-a-half-hour drive. The problem was not knowing if that was where Meredith was going, or if that was where she had been.

I sighed. "Marsha, did you bring any hiking gear?" Like it or not, the campgrounds were our only lead.

Chapter Twenty-Two
Survivalists

My last hiking trip began with me escaping after being seized by Paulo Bellagio and his lackey. The middle of the trip offered some highlights as it forced Cade and me to work together to save Dylan. Toward the end there was a shootout, and the final result was three people, me included, being carried out on stretchers. I was getting nauseated just thinking about it.

"Marsha, we need to stop and get some snacks."

"We had lunch before we left. Reach behind the seat and get an orange if you're still hungry."

I started gagging.

"Are you okay?"

"Yes, it's just my nerves and the thought of all that acidity in the orange made me feel worse. The same thing happened before I went to Galveston. I assumed I was over the panic attacks and queasiness from the abductions, but evidently I'm not." I took deep breaths to fight the nausea.

"Let's get your mind off that topic then." She smiled a mischievous grin. "Dylan found an interesting way to apologize. He sent me a few texts. Mostly pictures, but some were accompanied with interesting narratives. Guaranteed to take your mind in a different direction. Although I'd feel a bit guilty showing them to you, with you being in your celibate state and all."

"That's not exactly a true statement."

"Define 'not exactly' and you know I'm a slow learner, so I'll need lots of examples and details."

I was happy to oblige, beginning with the afternoon shoe salesman roleplay, then moving on to Sticks's and my version of ride 'em cowboy. I ended with the afterglow ruining moment, also known as the contraceptive question.

"But I thought you were on the pill?" Marsha asked.

"Only for two weeks and I haven't followed all the directions. I started the package before I started my period. I was two days late but didn't want to wait another week to begin taking them."

"I can see why you did it, but what did the doctor say?"

"I never went to the doctor. I had a prescription left over from my Peter phase."

Peter Johnson was my ex-fiancé. He was also a philanderer and a fraud, along with being my motivation to become a private investigator. I had met him at Baylor University. He was wealthy, handsome, and seemed to have a bright future with a supportive family. That was a lifetime ago.

"Lainee, we've been friends since middle school, and that includes the embarrassing reproductive class in eighth grade. I know you know better. Safe sex was drilled into our heads and Mrs. Hendrickson was fired because she didn't teach only abstinence. We pledged in her honor not to have unprotected sex. You know I disregard most of your rules and regulations, but that is one I've upheld, and I'm surprised you didn't."

"At the time, my mind was a little muddled. I was thinking more along the lines of marital versus premarital sex not protected versus unprotected when the act occurred."

"What has been going on with you? I haven't seen you check items off of any lists lately and until today, I can't even remember the last time you made one."

"I'm starting out on my own, Marsha. For the first time in my life, I'm not worrying about my father's legal reputation or my mother's disappointment. I was always so regimented, but all of that structure didn't stop chaos from coming. I'm trying to change my outlook."

"You're also starting to stray from your Grandmother's values. That used to be one of my biggest wishes, but now it's the brightest warning sign. Should I be staging an intervention?"

I began getting queasy again. "This conversation is making me want to go back to the dark side. I almost told you I'd help you plan the intervention." Pointing to a store along the road, I said, "There's a shop. I need something to settle my stomach."

Marsha pulled into a mom and pop outdoorsman store that relied on scare tactic survivalist advertising. Those advertisements did not help alleviate my panicky mode either.

Thanks to the generosity of Marsha's father, who still pays her living expenses, and to her grandmother, who left Marsha a sizable trust fund, we left with a rather large purchase. Part of our acquisitions included dehydrated ration packs, gallons of water to hydrate said rations, a pocketknife with accessory gadgets, and a high-powered flashlight, among other things. Best of all was the rented satellite phone with solar charging battery.

For convenience, we also got a two-person tent that could be inflated using a portable air pump, included in the package at a small additional cost. The bottom of the tent converted into a blow-up, full-sized mattress. These might seem like extravagant purchases, but after my previous escapades through rough terrain, along with information from the survivalist video the owner showed us, I viewed them almost as necessities.

Chapter Twenty-Three
Degrees, Minutes, and Seconds

Marsha and I drove to the Mooreland Campground. The online overview campsite guide I was looking at, right before all cell service ended, stated Mooreland had picnic areas, some pay by night camping pads, and, hallelujah, restroom facilities were also available. We chose it over the barebones Lincoln Tract, which was a free campsite. Unfortunately, I had not clicked on the actual link or I would have known the facilities were a solitary pit-dug toilet with a structure built around it to protect privacy. Nothing, however, could protect one from the stench.

Disappointed with our campground decision, we took off along a trail to hopefully find a better restroom option.

Marsha had found cover off the trail behind a fallen tree and began taking care of necessities.

I stood as guard and scanned the mountainous landscape. "The view is amazing, but I don't know how we're going to find Meredith. It's just too immense." I got out the digital binoculars and turned them on, playing with the features. There was a screen that recorded the area you were focusing on instead of having to squint through the lenses, which were functional in case the battery was running low or the screen couldn't be used because of glare or brightness. "This is like watching high definition television, Marsha." I fiddled around with it some more and it began beeping. I looked at the display.

Current Coordinates:
035°45'24.10"N
105°39'40.87"W

Marsha completed her task and stood beside me. "We've only been here twenty minutes and I already feel grimy."

I reached into my newly acquired all-purpose fanny pack and gave Marsha a wet wipe to disinfect her hands before relinquishing the binoculars to her.

"You had wipes? They could have been better used a few minutes ago."

I shrugged as she began scanning the range.

"We need to get to the campsite, Marsha. I think I know where to find Meredith."

As we neared the car, we heard voices, a high-pitched hum, a few grunts, a thud, then a louder curse. When we cautiously rounded the bend, I was once again surprised to see Ronaldo. This time, he was leaning against the front of the rental. One man was inflating our tent. It was flopping in the slight breeze. The air pump sounded like it was on its last breath as it struggled to fill the tent completely. The high-pitched noise was now close to a screech and blocked out any sounds we were making.

Two other men were setting up a camper trailer. It was one we had looked at in the survivalist store. With the push of a few buttons, this camper would unfold into temporary living quarters for four. The two men were leveling and adjusting the supports of the trailer before expanding it.

Even though we had approached unheard, we were not unseen. A woman stepped out of the parked SUV that I had assumed was empty.

"Stop," was all she said.

The only movement was the solo guy turning off the air pump and all four men turning to look at Marguerite Bellagio. I had seen photos of her on a TV crime show documentary, but the images had not captured her commanding presence.

Her black hair was knotted at the neck with her long mane wrapped in front to flow over her left shoulder. She wore white flared pants, and a gold undershirt with a white blazer. Most of her face was covered with oversized sunglasses, which made her large, looped gold earrings stand out even more. On her right hand, she wore rings of varying widths on her index finger and thumb. The first knuckle of her ring finger was encompassed by a pink, marquise-cut diamond ring. Her left hand remained unadorned with the exception of the loose gold link watch band that hung down the back of her hand. As she took a step forward, I could see she was wearing white kitten-heeled sandals. She looked ill dressed for the environment.

It took me a moment to realize Marsha and I had also obeyed her directive and were staring, waiting for our next prompt.

The men resumed their duties as she spoke directly to Marsha and me. "Why would you come to such a forsaken land?"

My trance broke and my confidence was bolstered. She showed insecurity by questioning the location. I was superior to her in the camping and hiking arena, especially after surviving my previous wilderness encounter. I chose not to think about my probable inferiority when compared to the men all around me setting up the equipment. "Before answering your question, I need to know how you knew we were here." My gaze turned to Ronaldo.

He looked sheepish again. "I put a tracking device on your earring. We've been following you ever since you left."

I took off my earrings, noticed the microscopic black dot sticker, and threw them to the ground.

As I raised my leg to crush them with my heal, Ronaldo yelled, "No, wait! Do you know how expensive those things are?"

"Don't whine about money, cousin. It's pathetic."

Ronaldo closed his mouth and once again leaned on the car.

"We came here because my husband was abducted and we're looking for him." I walked to our rental. The back doors were opened, and I noticed a fourth henchman on the ground putting together the heating and cooking equipment we had purchased. I didn't complain. If the car was going to be broken into, this was the best possible scenario.

Marsha reached for her phone. "I'm calling the police."

I tugged at the sleeve of her shirt. "There's no cell service. You'd have to use the satellite phone. Besides, I don't think we need to get law enforcement involved just yet."

Marsha groaned.

Marguerite smiled. "I thought you said this woman was a simpleton, Ronaldo. Those are the smartest words one can ever hear."

Ronaldo knelt in front of me. "Your shoe's untied. Here, let me get that for you. I don't want you to trip."

I looked at my shoes. The laces were tied. "Not going to fall for that a third time, Ronaldo." From the backseat of the rental, I grabbed my purse along with the bag of clothing and hiking boots we had purchased from the store earlier. "Let's go change, Marsha." I wasn't going to take the chance of any article of clothing I was wearing being tagged with a GPS tracker.

"Hey, we can be creative and make room for three," one of the henchmen yelled out.

"Don't think so," Marsha replied tersely crawling in the tent behind me.

"I don't have to join in. You could leave the tent open so we can watch."

I didn't speak or look at the man. I gave him my answer by simply zipping the tent flap closed.

Once we were alone in the tent, we got out of our city-girl clothes, changing into our more practical, newly acquired hiking clothes.

I whispered, "I know where Caitlynn and Meredith are. The trick is finding a way to get to them without alerting our visitors."

"I thought you trusted them."

"Despite what Ronaldo said, I don't think Marguerite has turned over a new leaf. I trust them with me because Marguerite is grateful to me only. I don't trust them with you or with the daughter of a federal agent." I pulled out a journal of lists from my purse, opening it and pointing to my copy of the calculations from Meredith's filebox. "Look. I think these are social security numbers, but the answer isn't correct. I think it's coordinates written in degrees, minutes, and seconds."

"How do you know these things?"

I unzipped the window flap at the back of the tent, took out the small pocketknife we had purchased, then cut the clear plastic covering. "I learned about it when I substituted in a world geography class."

"Did you learn evasive tactic maneuvers?"

Unfortunately, my answer was, "No."

***

"Remind me why you wanted to come here and not tell anyone where we were going?" Marsha hissed as we squatted behind a hollow log.

"Probably for the same reason you decided to

listen to me," I hissed in return. I made a slashing motion with my hand, sending the message for her to be quiet. "You're echoing. We don't want them to be able to hear us. They're only a few feet away."

"We're using binoculars, Lainee. So yes, they are just a few feet away. From that rock. Which is about 150 yards from us."

We were looking at two men standing behind Meredith and Caitlynn under the cover of a thicket of trees. The females were sitting back to back, but neither were gagged nor bound. I suppose the situation could be innocent. Maybe the girls had needed a break and the men's fierce looks were due to the frustration of having to stop. That could have been true if you subtracted the women's terrified looks from the equation. Of course, you would also have to eliminate the third man who was digging a hole.

Chapter Twenty-Four
Mike, Kenny, Charles, and Sid

Looking at Meredith and Caitlynn then, I wished I did have special tactical training. I had no idea how to help them.

Marsha was trying to figure out how to use the satellite phone. We were now seeing the flaw in our logic of waiting to watch the YouTube instructional video. If we could have gotten enough signal to watch a video, we wouldn't have needed a SAT phone.

A helicopter flew over in the distance. "You stay here and get the phone working. I'm going to get closer while the helicopter drowns out the noise."

I did a cross between a duck-walk and a hunchback gait, hoping I looked more adept than I felt. As I got closer, I could hear whimpering. It sounded like Meredith, too deep for a young teenager. I could also hear the men speaking but couldn't make out any words, until a simply stated, "Please." That must have been Caitlynn. Then a scream.

I inched closer and took the risk of standing to look above the overgrown brush. One of the men had grabbed Meredith by the throat. "Where're they, bitch? We're not diggin' for nothin'. If we don't find the bonds, this'll be yer graves."

Meredith was gasping, grappling with the hand at her throat, trying to get him to release her.

The second man spoke. Both of the men had Irish accents but were of the dialect that made Hilda turn her nose up. "Mike. Let 'er go. She knows the stakes. Besides, we aren't gonna kill the girl. We'll hold 'er for leverage against the old man. If that dudn't work, she'll get a good price on the market."

Mike let Meredith fall to the ground. She and Caitlynn embraced.

"Damn lawyer husband, tryin' ta double cross the boss. He shoulda known better," Mike said as he spit on Meredith.

The hostages cowered together, crying and comforting each other.

Mike knelt in front of them. Meredith moved to shield Caitlyn.

"Listen ta the cryin'. And smell the fear." Mike mocked them. He sniffed the air and beat his chest, reminding me of a gorilla showing aggression. "God, I love it. Almost as much as hearin' 'em beg." He stroked Meredith's cheek. "That'll be soon, lil darlin'."

To Meredith's credit, she met his gaze with strength, denying him the pleasure of intimidation.

Words weren't working, so Mike simply changed tactics. He pulled out a knife and examined it closely. "I missed a spot," He touched it to his tongue and licked. "I love the taste o' blood." He smiled. "Especially the old lady's blood. You shouldn't have run. I woulda found you instead o' havin' ta torture an old lady. She sure begged." Mike examined the knife again. "But after enough cuttin', she led us ta you. And the Fed."

So, these were the people who killed Mara and abducted Sticks.

The third man stood upright. "Found somethin'."

Mike jumped into the knee-deep, oblong hole then bent over, hoisting a leather messenger bag into the air. Opening it, he pulled out documents. "These're them."

The second man tried to grab the papers, but Mike won the tug of war, and placed the strap of the bag around his neck and over one of his shoulders. He then picked up the shovel, using it to bear weight as he climbed out of the hole.

Unexpectedly, he lifted the shovel, swinging it into the back of Meredith's head. Blood began gushing. Meredith slumped forward, unmoving.

Caitlynn screamed. I put my hand over my mouth and bit down hard to stifle my own and swallowed the bile that threatened to escape. Retching would call attention to my presence and also put Marsha in danger. My head was spinning, fingers tingling. I was worried I might pass out. With everything that I had gone through, this was the first time I felt pure evil emanating from a person.

Mike extracted the blade of the shovel that had been imbedded in Meredith's skull and kicked her. She rolled into the pit. "Charles, cover her up. Kenny, grab the girl. We gotta get movin'."

The men and Caitlynn began walking in the opposite direction, with Caitlyn struggling, looking back toward her mother.

Marsha made her way to me. "Oh, my god. Did we just witness a murder?" Her fingernails dug into my upper arm, her face pale. Her breath became shallow.

I wrapped my arm under hers as support, helping her to the ground, worried she may be the one to pass out. I needed to think quickly to get us out of the situation. I couldn't be responsible for another death. Dylan was right. Marsha shouldn't have come to help me. I would have apologized to her, but I wasn't going to have her lose confidence in me by reminding her that I had previously made bad decisions.

"Marsha, I need the SAT phone." I pried it from her hands, praying I'd be able to figure out how to use it. "We need back up."

Several snapping twigs could be heard as the brush was trampled behind us. I moved in front of Marsha, bending to pick up a stick. Three men emerged from the bush. "You have backup." Ronaldo approached us, followed by two of the lackeys.

Anger replaced my fear. "You! How did you find us?"

"Tracker in your boot."

"But I changed shoes. You couldn't have."

"I put it in the boots while they were still in the bag in the car. I acted like I put it on the shoes you were wearing to make sure you changed."

I stared in disbelief.

"The words you're looking for here are thank you."

I conceded, somewhat begrudgingly. "Thank you."

"And we've already contacted the park ranger service and the local police."

"What happened to the 'smartest words are don't contact the authorities' statement?"

"That policy was abandoned once they," he pointed to the two men behind him, "recognized who we're dealing with."

I turned to the burly men and pointed toward Meredith. "Can you guys go check on her now? There may be a chance she's still alive."

The two henchmen looked at each other, trying to determine if, or which one, should tell me the truth I already knew. Deciding against either, they shook their heads and moved toward the newly dug hole. Their movements startled Charles, who threw down the shovel and ran in the direction of his cousins.

When they were busy uncovering the body, Marsha asked Ronaldo, "Who were those men and what did they do to make the Bellagios scared of them?"

"They're cousins of Sid Foley, an Irishman who made a fortune as an underling in the IRA. He moved to America with the money he was supposed to have used to purchase explosives. His lack of scruples helped him climb the financial ladder over here. A guy like him doesn't let zoning laws, environmental issues, or people get in the way of his projects."

The irony of a cousin of one of the biggest crime lords in Chicago telling this story with such disdain was not lost on me. I wondered how he justified the actions of Marguerite and her employees.

"There were lots of casualties when he came into Chicago and took over the Fiero territory. Most of them were carried out by Mike and Kenny, or Micheil and Cainnech, as they're known in Ireland."

"What about the third guy?"

"Carlus—he hates to be called that, prefers Charles—is the cleaner. He comes in when they need a heavy hitter. He may not be as smart, but he is just as heartless. Although none of them come close to Sid in terms of brutality. The Bellagios know who not to mess with and aren't going to start a full out war with those guys."

I didn't want to start a war either, but I couldn't let them take Caitlynn. "I've got to go now or I'll lose them."

"You follow, you're on your own. We can't get involved. Don't destroy the tracker this time. It'll help the authorities find you. That's all the assistance we can provide."

I nodded my head, understanding what Ronaldo was telling me.

I turned to Marsha. "We have to update the FBI. Let's get the phone to work." We both looked at it, trying to identify the purpose of each button.

"Oh, for God's sake, it's not that difficult." Ronaldo took the phone from me, pushed a button, and it came to life, ready to allow us to communicate with the outside world. "Number?"

Marsha and I looked dumbfounded and I got the feeling we were doing a great impersonation of Lucy and Ethel. I couldn't help it. I was incapable of thinking clearly at that time.

Marsha took out her cell and rattled off Dylan's phone number. Once it began ringing, Ronaldo handed the phone to me. "Leave us out of it."

Dylan answered on the first ring.

"Gainess."

"Dylan, it's Lainee. I'm with Marsha and we're okay."

Dylan blew out a breath. "Good to hear, but I don't have much confidence in that statement considering you called from an unknown number."

"We're at the Moreland campground in New Mexico and there may be a dead body."

"It's not Torres, is it?"

"No, it's his girlfriend from high school, Meredith Bennett." I could feel the tension release from Dylan, even through the phone. "She was killed by a guy named Mike Foley. He and his cousins were looking for some bonds. They still have Sticks's daughter."

"Is this Mike Foley the cousin of Sid Foley? Was he there? Did you or Marsha make your presence known to him?" Dylan's tone was even, but the rapid-fire questioning gave away his panic.

"Sid wasn't here." I could hear clicking in the background over the phone as I spoke. "It was Mike, Charles, and Kenny. They didn't see us."

"I typed the campground into the system. An

anonymous tip was called in earlier. Park Rangers have already been sent. It'll help that they have this information. Those men are extremely dangerous. They've been to the strip club once. I can't tell you what happened, but they make the Bellagios look like altar boys."

"I understand." This confirmed my suspicion that Dylan's side job as an exotic dancer was actually an undercover assignment. "They are also responsible for the murder of a lady Sticks and I interviewed in Albuquerque, Mara Merriwether. Plus, they have Sticks."

"Lainee, you keep Marsha away from those men. Don't let her play your sidekick while you're playing the hero."

"I'll make sure she doesn't interact with them." I knew that he implied I should stay with Marsha while keeping her safe, but he hadn't actually said it, so I had every intention of being able to follow through on my word.

"Good." I thought Dylan was going to disconnect, instead he said, "Wait! Did you say Torres had a daughter?"

"Yes. With Meredith. She's from Phoenix." I shifted on my feet, wanting to get off the phone. "I don't have time to get into all the details. Please just make sure help is coming." I disconnected before he could say anything else, handed the phone to Marsha, and turned in the direction the men had headed.

Marsha blocked my path. "Lainee, let this go. You saw what they did to the mother right in front of her daughter."

"I can't live with myself knowing I didn't do everything I could to save Caitlynn."

Marsha grabbed my elbow. "Wouldn't living with guilt be better than dying?"

"No, it wouldn't." Knowing she couldn't change my mind, I hugged her, then turned to Ronaldo. "I consider this woman part of my family. I know that tie is important to you. I'm asking you to protect her like you would me. This is how Marguerite can repay me."

Ronaldo nodded his head and stepped beside Marsha. I turned my back to them and walked quickly before I lost the worst guys. I couldn't believe I was leaving Marsha with the bad ones.

Chapter Twenty-Five
No Lingering

I had no trouble following their path. There were crushed blades of grass, broken stems and branches, along with footprints, mapping out their journey. I stopped suddenly when I heard yelling.

"How could you be so stupid? You weren't even wearin' gloves."

"We're in the middle of nowhere. I tho' it was an animal."

"When I call ya in, yer job is to dig deep or dismember, not to be runnin' off when a noise scares ya."

The argument continued as the voices got closer. They were retracing their steps to the clearing. Back toward Marsha. I regretted, yet again, that I had put her in harm's way.

I did the only thing I could. I continued walking toward the men. It was only moments before I encountered them.

Mike was still carrying the satchel of papers he deemed more important than Meredith's life.

"Well, well, well."

Three words had never terrified me as much as those had. Or it might possibly have been Mike's accompanying smile that didn't quite reach his eyes. They were a cesspool. Unreadable. Evil.

I looked at Caitlynn. She looked even more frightened than before. Her thick, dark hair was cut shoulder length and layered around her face. Parts of it were stuck to her tear-streaked, dirt-smeared face. Other than her initial glance in my direction, showing eyes very similar to Clint's, she avoided any contact. I knew she saw me as another victim, not as her rescuer.

I walked around the men. They weren't in the least threatened by me and seemed curious as to what I was going to do while they allowed me free reign, for the moment anyway. Mike still wore the heartless smile. Kenny stood with his arms crossed and Charles was grateful he was no longer the target of Mike's anger.

I hugged Caitlynn. "You look so much like your father."

Mike grabbed my arm, spinning me around in the process. He didn't say a word before hitting me on the left cheek. If he hadn't been holding onto my arm, I would have fallen to the ground.

I could not believe the excruciating pain. I felt dizzy. Caitlynn's screams echoed through my muddled mind.

"That's the bitch who pulled the gun on us. Guess the FBI bastard can watch us sell off 'is daughter and kill 'is wife." Kenny was laughing as he spoke. As frightening as that was to hear, it was also a relief to know Sticks was alive.

Charles spoke up, "Yes, but we're gonna have fun with 'er first."

Mike let go of me. I fell as he sucker punched his cousin in the gut. "You won't be havin' any fun. Go back, do yer job, and find some way to make it to the rendezvous point. You're on yer own. If she's here, others are or will be soon. I'm not goin' down with ya and yous know better than to try to take me down with ya."

Mike turned and towered over me, smiling his hideous smile. "The fun starts now." Then he hit me twice more.

***

I heard a faint voice coming in waves as if through layers of water.

I tried to focus. No. I wasn't in water. I could breathe, although I found I didn't want to. My chest throbbed as the added pressure of taking in air sent shards of pain throughout my torso.

There was the voice again, seemingly drifting in and out.

I lifted my head, trying to pinpoint the origin of the sound. Nausea struck without warning. I laid back down, taking in a deep breath to fight the urge to throw up, instantly regretting it as the discomfort once again reminded me of probable broken ribs.

I gave in to the nausea and turned on my side to vomit. This time, a burn radiated through my shoulders and up to my wrists, which were bound together and raised above my head. Still heaving, I felt as though I would die.

After ejecting the contents of my stomach, my head spun at a much slower rate. I took a chance and opened my eyes—or eye, singular in this case, as one was swollen shut—discovering I was on a mattress. It was covered only with a plastic tarp. Droplets of blood and vomit were standing or dripping in rivulets on the tarp. There were no sheets, blankets, or comforter. The stench of bile made me gag again.

I looked up, trying to focus on one spot to avoid vomiting once more. Looking overhead, I noticed my wrists were in cuffs and chained to the headboard. There was enough slack for me to move but the weight was too heavy for me to change positions. I feared I may have rebroken my arm.

The voice returned, more clearly this time.

Slowly turning to my right, I could see a second bed. Caitlynn was on it. Her bed, however, was made perfectly. The pink, ruffled comforter with sheer drapes canopying overhead would be dream bedding for any little princess. As innocent as it looked, there was something sinister about the decor. Caitlynn was curled in a ball on the middle of the bed, rocking back and forth. She had been cleaned and dressed in pleated white pajamas with pink hearts. Her hair was styled in doggy ears.

My heart sank as I silently prayed nothing physical had happened to her. It was her voice I had been hearing. She kept repeating, "Please, God, get us out of here."

I interrupted her imploring prayer. "Caitlynn, what happened? You okay? What did they do?" My lips were swollen, making it difficult for me to speak.

"They only took pictures and made a video of me eating and reading." She began quietly weeping. "They were talking like I was being sold. I'm so scared of what's going to happen."

"Be found before then. Took your father, too. FBI agent. People looking for us." I wondered how much she could understand me. Talking was taking an extraordinary amount of energy.

"I don't even know that person. My dad is the man who got my mom killed. Why is this happening?"

I shook my head. Not having the answers for her was difficult.

"Shh! I hear footsteps. They're coming back. Pretend you're asleep. Every time you move, they hit you and they film it."

I partially closed my eyes as the doorknob turned, looking through my lashes.

One man came in with food for Caitlynn. Before giving it to her, he arranged a video camera.

"Here, lass, you gotta eat up. You gonna want to keep yer strength for where ye're going." This man had a stronger Irish accent. He was rugged with stringy hair and leathered skin. He seemed less educated than Mike and Kenny.

"What about her?" Caitlynn pointed at me. "She needs to keep her strength, too. Can you leave some food for when she wakes up?"

"Aww, that's sweet o' you, little lass, but it's best to not let 'er linger. She's not long for this world. Her only purpose now is to torment the husband." The man paused. Even though his back was turned to me, I could imagine him crossing himself as I had seen Hilda do many times before. "I'd do 'er in now but the big bosses would be mad that I spoiled their fun." He seemed like a sweet man, except for the fact that he was offering to kill me.

Walking to the camera again, the man stated, "Stop askin' questions. Ya gotta eat. I'm supposed to film ya." He fumbled with the video equipment. "Used to be we could live feed the videos, but the coppers're gettin' better at trackin' 'em now." He continued, mumbling more to himself than speaking to us. "Sure givin' me too much ta do. Runnin' me all over the country while they collectin' they're dolls. Ev'ry city they in, I gotta follow."

I took a moment to process what he was saying. If my desire to seek justice against these men for Meredith was strong, it was forged tenfold to get justice for or possibly save some of the other dolls he was referring to. The roiling in my stomach returned, this time as a sickening feeling of how many countless others were going, or had gone, through the same nightmare at the hands of these men.

The man turned on the camera then began rummaging through something behind me. I could hear a cabinet creak and a drawer sliding opened and closed. He came over to my bed and spread a blanket over me. He was a man with a conscience. I might be able to use that to Caitlynn's and my advantage. At least I thought that until he explained his actions. "Don't wanna let 'er get too cold. We need to have 'er warm ta confuse the coppers on time o' death."

After he finished his duties, the man removed the digital card from the camera and left the room, locking the door behind him. Either as an oversight, another confusion tactic, or as an act of compassion—I wasn't abandoning his good side yet—he forgot to take the remainder of Caitlynn's food.

Staying silent through the twinges sent throughout my chest cavity when breathing, along with observing the situation, had been exhausting. I didn't realize I had drifted off until I felt a light tapping on my leg, the only place on my body that wasn't throbbing.

Chapter Twenty-Six
Buyers

"Lainee? Lainee? Wake up. Come on, I can't do this alone. We need to stick together."

I opened my one good eye.

"Thank God, you're alive. You stopped moaning. I thought you might have died." Caitlynn slumped with relief then bolstered herself, straightening almost immediately as she held out a spoon with mushed fruit on it. "Can you chew? I mashed it as much as I could."

I opened my mouth what felt like a mile but Caitlynn had to dabble the food into it because the spoon wouldn't fit. The cantaloupe, honeydew, and strawberry mixture tasted glorious and helped quench my thirst as well. My stomach growled, and I wondered how much time had passed since I'd last eaten.

"Where are we? What day is it?"

"We're in a hotel room because I can hear other people walking by. I yelled out once, but those men must be close because the smaller guy came in and started hitting you."

"Kenny?"

"Yes, that's his name. He said if I did it again they were going to start cutting little pieces off you. Then he told me he'd do the same to anyone who would come in to help." She continued giving me spoonfuls of food as she spoke. "This is the fourth meal. I think they're feeding me twice a day, so it's been about two days."

Caitlynn could roam the room. She got up and went into the restroom, coming back with a washcloth to wipe my chin. "Who exactly are you? The man who killed my mom came in with a video of my real dad. He was tied to a metal chair with his hands behind him. It didn't look like they'd hurt him though."

I opened my mouth wider for another bite and was rewarded with a shooting pain from the hinge of my jaw to the base of my neck.

"What should I call him? When my mom told me about him, she said his name was Clint."

I shook my head to confirm her statement and to get her to move along in the story.

"Anyway, they were facetiming you being beaten. He went ballistic, trying to jump at them and kept calling out Lainee. That's how I found out your name."

For two more days, Caitlynn and I saw no one but the old man bringing food. Each visit he was surprised to find me alive. He never filmed me which made me wonder if Sticks had been killed. Caitlynn had only seen Mike and Kenny before I awoke. Since they hadn't been back, I hadn't been beaten again. Charles was a no show. I assumed he hadn't been able to meet the others as they had planned.

The standard practice of Caitlynn feeding me her leftovers then me resting continued. I was getting stronger and moving more often and with better ease. Occasionally, we would talk. She was very curious about her father. The questions she asked made me curious about him as well. I found out exactly how little I knew about him.

The pattern altered when the old man came in with a change of clothes for Caitlynn instead of food.

"''Ey, little lass. Time ta spruce ya up. Auction was last nigh'. Ya be meetin' ya owner in about an hour."

Caitlynn looked terrified. My heart began racing faster. I needed to make a plan to get us out of here. Time was running out quickly.

"Change in ta these and don't be tryin' nothin'." He placed the clothes she needed to wear on the bed. "If'n I have to hit ya, you'll get some bruises an' you don't wanna give yer owner any ideas about hurtin' ya. Sometimes they be likin' a fighter, but that makes it a lot worse fer ya. Jus' relax, maybe think a somethin' else when he introduces hisself to ya."

He turned around to allow her to change. This was our chance. Caitlynn grabbed the plastic pink princess castle used as decoration on her nightstand. She wasn't able to swing before there was a slight knock on the door. The old man moved to answer it.

"You're late." He greeted the woman at the door in a terse manner. This woman had spiky bleached hair and wore heavy make-up. Her cheek was marred with long scratches.

The man stroked her cheek. "What happened to ya, Linda?"

"College girl fought us," the woman answered in a New York accent. "Her owner dropped out. Second one. They're tired of messing with her. She's going to the dual keeper auction. If she makes it through, she's going to wish she hadn't."

The man crossed himself and kissed the medallion he wore around his neck then turned to speak to Caitlynn. "This what I been talkin' 'bout. Don't put yerself in her place." He looked puzzled when he saw the toy in Caitlynn's hand. He grabbed it from her and pulled her hair, throwing her down onto the bed. "Don't be tryin' nothin' on me, lass. I ain't been givin' ya no reason to hurt me."

The woman touched his upper arm, gently tugging on it.

His angered lessened and he said, "Listen, yer gonna change clothes. Ya can either do it yerself or I'm gonna haf ta do it fer ya."

Linda was grandmotherly and stepped between Caitlynn and the man, elbowing him out of the way. "Cyrus, be quiet. She has reason to hate everyone because no one's helping her." She assisted Caitlynn to sit up. "We all have our reasons for not fighting back, deary. I can't help you get out of here, but I'll help make it easier on you. First, let's let you get a shower. You always feel better when you're cleaned up."

The woman led her to the restroom. I could hear the shower running.

This was my chance to get Cyrus on my side.

"Please, let her escape. All you have to do is turn

the other way. Let her walk out. I don't understand why you're doing these things. You have an inner voice that you are fighting with every time you walk in or out of here."

Cyrus turned his back to me, beginning to fold the bedding and pack away the decorations. I shuddered to think of when they would be used again as he quietly said, "Ya know not'in' about me, lass. Don' be actin' like ye do."

"It's in your eyes, Cyrus. They tell me everything. You have regrets."

"My only regret is letting 'em find out I have a daughter. I'm working off my debt to get 'er out."

"So, you're allowing them to do to others what they are doing to your daughter?"

Cyrus sat on the now stripped bed. "It's not that easy, lass. My daughter is still in their care. She has it much worse. I 'ave to get 'er out of there. I only have to work for them three more months."

"How many do they take each month? I know they have at least two now. You have to stop this. So many lives are being torn apart. You can make a difference."

Standing up, he turned away from me and said, "Can't do it, missy." He once again began organizing the items.

"Did you know that girl in there is the daughter of an FBI agent? You let her escape, they will help you find yours."

He stopped what he was doing to listen.

I continued, "We can make it look believable. Hit

you over the head or something."

Cyrus turned slightly toward me, but it was too late. The door opened.

Mike and another man, probably the auction winner, walked inside. The man looked much different than I had anticipated. I expected a foreigner, maybe Middle Eastern, from a country where women were repressed. Possibly an unattractive person. Definitely someone who exuded evil. What I saw was a tall, blond man in a business suit. Someone I would feel comfortable talking to at a nightclub or party.

"Get the girl." Mike demanded.

"She's still getting ready." Cyrus cowered in the presence of Mike. I knew there was no way he would help me now.

"I didn't ask what she was doing. I said to get her."

"Wait," I pleaded. "Please, don't do this."

Mike slapped me. My face stung, but I felt the impact throughout my body. I felt light-headed and the queasiness returned in full force.

The blond man spoke, "Who's this? I may have a buyer who's interested in her. He likes it rough and snuffs them."

I lifted my head, looking at the man through the hair draping around my face. He must be a go-between. His assessing look made me wonder how I missed the evil lurking beneath his professional veneer.

"Get the old man to film her and upload the video." He pulled out his phone. "If my client wants her, I'll expect a bonus in addition to my finder's fee and commission."

"No way," Mike growled.

"Yes, you will pay a bonus. Think of it as a convenience fee for not having to dispose of a body."

The men silently stared at one another. The blond calmly leaned against the desk crossing his ankles, giving Mike time to decide. Mike's body tensed. His anger rising. I was closest to him and feared he would strike out against me. He raised a fist.

"Uh, uh, uh. The only person touching her from now on will be my client."

Their standoff ended when Mike growled, "Cyrus, set up the camera."

My mind whirled. There was nothing I could do to rescue us, but if they took me with them, it might buy me some time to think of a plan.

The blond man began giving orders. "Lift her face. Get a close up of the bruises. Yes, he's going to love her." He was getting more excited with every command. I began to think there might not have been a client after all. "Yes, now lift her arm and drape the sheet over her. Let it play peekaboo with her breasts."

Mike did as he was told as Cyrus filmed. The heavy chain fell over his shoulder, which bore some of the weight and provided a respite for my aching muscles.

Cyrus crossed in front to shoot from various angles as Mike let my arm drop. Despite being outnumbered, I decided this was my chance. When my arm fell, the chain looped around Mike's neck. I simply pulled the chain tighter and rolled off the bed, taking Mike with me. He was gurgling, gasping for air, and clutching at the chain with both of his hands.

Linda and the man in the business suit hurriedly left. Cyrus stood staring. I got the feeling he was enjoying watching Mike struggle.

I pulled tighter as Mike rammed his head into my chest in an effort to make me loosen my grip. The pain was intense. My injured arm felt spliced and I feared the bone would pop and protrude with the amount of force I was exerting.

He was able to head butt me once, twice, then a third time. I was in agony. My ribs were piercing my lungs and I was having difficulty breathing.

I rolled over in an attempt to protect myself from the continuous battering. Mike released one hand from the chain, reaching up and grabbing my hair, lifting my head and slamming it into the floor. I curled around to give him less opportunity and areas to attack me. I rolled over and laid on top of the chain to apply more pressure. I could hear him wheeze, desperate for air. His efforts began to decrease as did his breathing. It was barely audible now.

I heard shuffling around me but was too weak to expend any energy discovering its source. My vision was blacking out, ears ringing. I was losing. I could only hope Mike would lose his battle first.

Chapter Twenty-Seven
Dreamland

The dreams were realistic but confusing.

The doctors were working on a woman.

They needed to stabilize her or she would lose her baby. I attempted to reach out to her, but my body wouldn't move. I spoke with heavy words that didn't fully form. No matter what I tried, my actions would not match my will to comfort her.

My mind darkened as the dream changed.

***

Sticks and Marsha were nurses. They were both in medical scrubs and surgical masks. Another doctor, in a white smock worn over scrubs, was talking to them.

"Despite all of her injuries, the baby's heartbeat is strong."

"Heartbeat? There's a heartbeat?" I would have expected Sticks to be elated at that news, but he seemed more dejected after hearing those words.

"Yes, but remember my earlier concerns. You can remain hopeful but need to consider the other alternatives we discussed."

After he shook both Sticks and Marsha's hands and left the room, Marsha asked, "You have a medical degree. What do you think?"

"I think he was being diplomatic."

"Diplomatic? He told us to expect the worst."

"He's trying to prepare us. I've seen this situation many times. It could go either way, but more times than not, it goes the way we don't want it to."

Marsha began crying quietly as Sticks put his arms around her. I wanted to hug them, too, but I couldn't get their attention.

Sticks loosened his grip on Marsha. "I should have said to hell with protocol and gotten there sooner instead of waiting for the tactical team. She might not be fighting for her life now."

"I wish you would have gotten there sooner, too. You know she is going to use this as a prime example of how she can take care of herself once she wakes up."

He faked a southern accent in a falsetto. "Oh, dear Lord, and Heaven help us."

"You know you sounded nothing like her. Your accent really sucks."

They hugged again, laughing this time. Marsha stepped out of the embrace. "I am thankful they could track the boot. If Mike had disposed of Lainee's clothing earlier, you may have never been found in time."

"Even though it led the cavalry to me, I wished it would have led them to Lainee first. It was hard waiting for Mike and Kenny to make their move after

I was rescued."

"What if they had gone underground?" Marsha shivered.

"Never underestimate the force greed and revenge has upon the actions of criminals, Marsha. Mike wasn't going to miss out on the money or the first-hand experience of selling an FBI agent's daughter. That was his downfall."

Marsha moved to the vinyl upholstered chair, scooted it closer to my bed, and sat down. "I do worry about when she wakes up. How do you think she'll react to killing someone?"

"I don't know. Maybe she won't think of it as taking a life. Hopefully, she'll see it as saving her and my daughter, plus the two other girls they were holding."

I felt the dream ending, but I didn't want to leave the scene. I felt sucked out and planted in a stranger one.

***

Marsha and Rad were the starring attractions as I was laying on my bed in my childhood bedroom. They were standing beside it, looking like they did in high school. Marsha was wearing her hair in a French braid. Rad had his hair longer and was in his letterman jacket. They were also arguing like they did in high school, except this time they were whispering instead of yelling at one another.

"How could you have done that to her?"

"Me? I wasn't the only one involved, Marsha. I was under the influence of the roofies, if you remember."

"Correction. You were recovering from being under the influence of the drug and you still should have known better."

"Why are you only blaming me? She had multiple, and I do mean multiple, opportunities to say no. Plus, I was responsible. I used protection."

"Then how did she get pregnant?"

"The last condom broke. It was probably old. I had found a stash in the bedside table at the bed and breakfast."

Marsha looked like she didn't believe him.

"Come on, Marsha. Even I don't carry three around in my wallet and who thinks to check for an expiration date. When I noticed the tear, I flipped. I thought about running scared, but on the drive home, I decided I didn't want to be like my dad." He sat down in the chair next to my bed. "The only thing I am guilty of is not telling her. After she went to sleep, I checked her phone calendar. You know how she tracks everything. I noticed it was two weeks since she'd had her period. It couldn't have been worse timing."

"Is that why you rented the basement apartment?"

"Yes, I thought I would be able to notice any signs and be there for her when she found out. Also, I did little things to protect the baby before she knew, like keep alcohol away from her and trying to make sure she got enough rest. I'd be there after it was born, too, and could help with all the feedings and everything. I never expected her to get married before we knew for sure. I thought maybe she did know and married that guy because she thought he was the dad. I was furious. Someone else wasn't going to be raising my kid. It pushed my inner asshole button."

"Please. You know it doesn't take much for that to come to the forefront."

"I'll admit, I didn't handle it well. I tried to hint that the child was mine to that Fed. He never picked up on it. It never occurred to me he didn't know and there was another reason they had gotten married."

He ran his fingers through his hair. His hair was so thick and long. My dad hated it. He didn't think Rad was respectable enough to date me.

Rad continued, "As much as I didn't want her to be pregnant, I don't want her to lose it either. And I feel so guilty because I know it is taking more out of her and she needs the energy to heal herself."

None of this was making sense. The dream was mixing memory with an absurd reality, making it almost believable. I was too exhausted to keep up with this dream and willingly drifted away.

Chapter Twenty-Eight
Wakey, Wakey

I awakened to bright lights and an incessant high-pitched beeping noise.

Marsha was fumbling with something on the edge of my bed, finding a cord and following it to the remote, where finally she pushed a button.

"She's waking up," Marsha turned her head to the left and said loudly to no one in the room.

Rad stuck his head through the door. "Do you want me to find a doctor?"

"You might as well make yourself useful. Everyone's already told you Lainee doesn't need a guard at the door. I don't know why you don't go back to Waco." Marsha lifted me slightly and plumped the pillows underneath. "You also didn't listen when everyone told you that you weren't wanted either."

"Not everyone, only you. And you need to remember that it was Clint who told me to come out. I'll leave when Lainee tells me to leave."

"If you want someone to tell you what to do, I'm your girl. Go get Agent Torres."

There were several reasons why I hadn't already told Rad to go. One, I had been either asleep or unconscious since before he arrived. Two, I couldn't speak because there was a tube down my throat. And three, he walked away, presumably to get Sticks, before I could relay the message.

"Yes. Can I help you?" Came a nasally voice through the speaker.

"My friend is awake. And this machine is going off."

"I'll let her nurse know."

"What happened?" I tried to say. I'm not sure what came out.

Marsha seemed to understand. She patted my hand as she spoke. "Don't talk. You had severe damage and swelling to the bronchial tubes aspirating on your vomit. Sticks was able to keep you going until the EMTs got there with an Ambu bag. The doctor had to intubate you once you got to the hospital." She gripped my hand.

I tried to speak again. The pain emanating from my throat was excruciating. I pulled at the tubes. My only thoughts were to get rid of the source of the pain. Marsha ran to the door, yelling for the nurse, almost mowing Rad down as he ran through it.

"Torres is on his way. I also told an RN at the nurse's station. I stayed until she contacted the doctor."

I was hearing everything but was having trouble processing.

Marsha tried to hold my hands down while calmly speaking to me, "Lainee, you have to calm yourself. There aren't many medication options to help you without harming the baby. Do you understand?"

I looked at Rad. His eyes were telling me things I

didn't want to hear. I was the pregnant woman from my dreams and Rad was the father.

I closed my eyes again. *Let me go back to sleep. Let me wake up to a different reality.*

***

There was movement in the room. I opened my eyes. Nothing had changed except Sticks had walked up behind Rad.

"Lainee, thank God." He reached around Rad to hold my hand.

Marsha walked to the other side of the bed to hold my other one as she said, "You gave us quite the scare." Her tone was overly bright, but tears were in her eyes.

I tried to mumble, "You're putting up quite the front," but the tube in my throat restricted my speech and the tape running down the side of my face holding the tube in place kept me from smiling. I wasn't sure what message I conveyed because my efforts to reassure them seemed to make them worry more.

Sticks moved Rad aside and began monitoring my vitals on the machine, pushing a button, making a printed readout emerge. Marsha began fiddling with my IV tubing, making sure nothing was kinked. Rad turned his back to me and walked a few steps away. I heard him blow out a breath and saw him run a hand through his hair.

Two nurses came in the room. The larger of the two said, "Dr. Torres, do we have to have another conversation about hospital privileges?"

He handed the readout to her. "I printed it out for you, Melba. It was merely a time saving consideration."

I loved how smooth my husband was, even if I couldn't say I loved him. Yet. I wonder what he thought about the baby. Why had he called Rad? Was he wanting to avoid the responsibility? Sticks would have the opportunity to raise this child, an opportunity he didn't have with Caitlynn.

Caitlynn. I waved my hand and tried to sit up. What had happened to her?

Melba touched my shoulder. "Mrs. Torres. Mrs. Torres. You need to be still."

I calmed and made a gesture of writing on one hand, hoping they would figure out I wanted paper and a pen. I was given a small white board and dry erase marker along with a washcloth to use as an eraser. I wrote: *How is Caitlynn?*

"You don't have any questions about yourself? You're hooked up to God knows how many machines and tubes, and the first question you ask is about my daughter? You are a special woman, Lainee." Sticks grabbed my hand and kissed my forehead. "Physically, she's come away with only a few scrapes, but she's being observed in the psychiatric unit."

I erased my question then wrote:

She needs support. 1) different father, 2) being on the run, 3) seeing mother killed, 4) 'dad' is a criminal, 5) hostage, 6) almost sold.

"I agree. I want to make sure she has all the

support she needs before facing her family in Arizona. I need to be with her when she does. She's being released tomorrow, Lainee. I won't be able to stay here while you recover."

That's alright. She took care of me. Now, you take care of her.

I erased once more and got everyone's attention. I wanted these next words to have an impact and get action. *Now, get this damned tube out of my throat!*

Marsha laughed. "Language, Lainee."

Rad said, "Yes! There's the Lainee I knew was in there."

Sticks turned to Melba. "We need the doctor in here. Get the orders to get this done."

Chapter Twenty-Nine
Alvin, Flo, and Peter

Trying to balance my inner peace with my warring memories of being held captive, I was transitioning from downward dog to cobra. The waterfall was flowing to provide a calming atmosphere. Marsha, wrapped in a blanket, sitting by the blazing fire pit to ward off the autumn chill, was there to provide rockiness and instability.

"How are you feeling? You've been so down since losing the baby."

"I would be feeling much better if people would stop asking me how I felt." After accepting the fact that I was pregnant, the baby had become my motivation to heal. We had made it through the ten-day hospital stay. But the morning after my release, I noticed a small pool of blood when I awoke and knew our journey together had ended. It was strange how something unexpectedly gained for a brief amount of time could cause such a feeling of loss.

"We ask mostly because we care and only partly because we don't believe you when you say you're fine."

"Glad to know trust is a vital part of our friendship."

"Our friendship is built on the premise that eventually I will wear you down, and at that time, I trust you will tell me the truth."

I gave up on doing yoga and sat beside Marsha on the overstuffed cushion of the outdoor wicker sofa. She held out the blanket, sharing it with me.

"Alright. Here goes. I won't deny that I was heartbroken after I lost the baby, but I'm feeling guilty because I also experienced an overwhelming sense of relief. In the hospital, I envisioned myself as a single mom who could take on any challenge. It made me feel stronger. But when those possible challenges no longer existed, a weight lifted. And the biggest relief was that I wasn't tethered to Rad anymore because of the baby."

"I hate to be the bearer of bad news, but you aren't going to be rid of him any time soon, Lainee. He did sign a year's lease."

"Don't remind me." I tucked the blanket under my chin and leaned into Marsha. "You were there when Sticks was told about the baby. Why did he call Rad?"

"They had done a blood test when you first arrived which showed you were pregnant. He was so excited, but when the doctor said the baby had a strong heartbeat, Clint's face went pale. He knew that meant your pregnancy was too far along and figured out right away that the timing fit in with your Galveston trip, not your after-dinner car ride. Rad made it obvious to Clint what had happened while you were together. Remember how you said you hadn't started your period before beginning the pill? There was a reason for that."

"That must have hurt Sticks. He wasn't able to raise Caitlynn and then to find out this one wasn't his baby."

We sat in silence for a few minutes. I changed the topic. "Sticks texted me late last night." I found the message on my phone and handed it over to Marsha. "Isn't that exciting! Maybe it will help my mood."

"A three-night vacation to a private beach with a handsome man who adores you? If that doesn't improve your outlook on life, you may need to consider psychiatric help."

"I may need to consider it anyway."

The back door opened as Hilda tentatively stepped out. "Lainee, there's someone here to see you."

I brightened my smile, telling myself to fake it until I could make it. I should have, however, waited to see who it was. My brother, Alvin, squeezed his way between Hilda and the door frame to come onto the patio, speaking into his cell phone. "Flo…Flo…" My sister kept speaking over him. He raised his voice. "Florence, I need to let you go. I'm here now. I'll let you know what she says." He disconnected and pulled an envelope from his inside jacket pocket. "What is this? Flo called my office in a fit to see if I'd heard about it. I've spent the last forty minutes convincing her you haven't lost your mind." I wasn't sure what he was referring to, but if my brother and sister were discussing it, it wasn't good news.

Hilda interjected for me. "That's an invitation,"

she said to him, then turned toward me. "Helga was busy planning the reception while ye were away, Lainee. The invitations went out just hours before we found out about your situation." Hilda could never bring herself to say the words abduction, kidnapping, or attack, preferring to gloss things over with the generic word 'situation.' With everything that had happened recently, I often had difficulty knowing which predicament she was referring to and for some reason, it upset her more when I asked her to clarify.

"Oh," was all I managed to say. "I had forgotten about that."

"How could you forget about your reception? Was it because it was for a wedding your brother and sister knew nothing about?"

"Alvin, calm down. I meant to tell you at the quarterly financial meeting."

"You mean the one you missed because you had been hospitalized, in ICU, after being beaten up by the Irish mob? And this was after you had been kidnapped months earlier by the Chicago mafia. That bit of information, was the headline story on the local news, which is how I found out about it."

"I'll admit I was planning to omit those parts of my story." Just like right then I omitted the detail that I also killed one of the Irish mob members. I hadn't been able to admit that out loud to anyone yet.

"You are making terrible decisions." Alvin continued. "As executor of mom's and dad's wills, I am stepping in to protect your investments."

"You can't do that. The will has already been

through probate."

"But your trust fund is still being managed by my firm."

"H-How…" I managed to sputter before my question died off as someone else stepped through the doorway. "Peter?" This day was getting even worse. I hadn't seen him since the day I'd called off our engagement before driving to my father's law offices with evidence of Peter's embezzlement. "Why are you here? Weren't you convicted of fraud?"

"I was, but only served six months. The rest of my sentence was commuted. One of the conditions of my parole is to do *pro bono* legal work to prove good moral character."

"If you had good moral character, I doubt you would have become a lawyer."

"Careful there, Lainee, your brother is a lawyer, not to mention your father was one as well." Peter smiled, his white teeth blinding on the dreary day. What I had once seen as polished, now seemed fake. For someone who had spent at least six months in prison, he wasn't any worse for the wear. His light brown hair was slicked back, and the suit he wore didn't have a wrinkle. He walked over and gave me an awkward hug. "I'll forgive the cold reception. I'm confident my visit wasn't listed on your daily agenda."

"How are you still practicing law? Wouldn't you have been disbarred?"

"Probably would have been if I had passed the bar before my sentencing. Getting it in jail was much easier than I thought. I had much more time to study without any distractions. It also looks better during a parole board hearing to become a lawyer while serving time."

Alvin interrupted. "Peter is here to help oversee your financial portfolio."

"Having Peter oversee my finances will jeopardize my finances."

"You jeopardize them, Lainee. I just received an invitation from you, announcing your marriage to a man no one even knew you were dating. Did you have him sign a pre-nup?"

"No."

"Exactly. You are your own worst nightmare, sis."

Alvin may have had a point. However, admitting it to him was another item that wasn't on my agenda for the day. "But why Peter?"

"Because I don't want to lose billable hours assigning this to an associate and his billable hours are free." He sat in one of the cushioned patio chairs as if the matter was settled. "Now, when can we meet your husband?"

I sighed, not wanting to admit the truth. "I don't actually have a husband."

Chapter Thirty
The Puppy in Its Place

My brother jumped to his feet. "What?!"

"Honestly, Alvin. It's reactions like this that make me not want to tell you what's going on in my life."

Hilda shuffled Peter and Marsha into the house. She had witnessed our sibling squabbles many times and knew it was best if they were done in private. Neither of us would back down if there was an audience.

"It's what's going on in your life that makes me have reactions like this. Between your ex-fiancé and whoever this," he looked at the invitation in his hand, "Clint character is, you are playing it wild with your future. Do you know how hard Dad and Mom worked and how much Flo and I sacrificed so your future could be secure?"

"Well, considering you're about to put my financial security into the hands of my ex-fiancé, I'm surprised you're throwing that one in my face. And what do you mean you and Flo sacrificed?"

"Lainee, do you honestly think that our parents' wealth was distributed evenly? Look at this house. What do you think it's valued at?"

"I haven't checked into it, but I know what it costs

to keep it running, and I know that you and Flo both got income-based inheritances, so yours keeps giving you money."

"Because we work for it, Lainee. You get to sit around the pool with your friends and pretend to play house with whichever guy comes along. You risk so much and aren't thankful for anything that has been provided for you."

"I work, too, Alvin, and I started my own business."

"Don't expect me to be proud of you for being a private investigator. Again, you're being reckless. You're like a puppy that craps all over the house then runs up to the master, wagging its tail, expecting to be praised."

"That's going too far."

"The problem with you is no one has ever gone far enough. We can't upset Lainee's delicate nature. We've all had to tiptoe around you ever since..."

"Don't say another word, Norman Alvin Delaney." Maybe he would get side tracked about me using his full name. I remembered constantly teasing him about it, and his initials, when we were younger, especially after he lost one of his testicles in a baseball injury. It seemed prophetic at the time.

He didn't get distracted. Instead, he said, "You're proving my point. You still can't tolerate any mention of the family's banned subject."

I wasn't going to stand idly by and let him harass me. "This is my home now, and you need to leave. I will be contacting my own lawyer to block anything you're trying to do with my trust fund." My stare was steady, but I inwardly rolled my eyes. I didn't know a single lawyer who wasn't associated with my brother.

"You will lose in that battle, Lainee."

"What I will do is take my chances."

He stood before me trying to once again intimidate me. I used to cower before these tirades of his. Now, I saw him as a pudgy, middle-aged, balding man, who looked like he should run along—or more appropriately walk very slowly—to get his blood pressure checked. His face was ruddy from anger and there was spittle on his chin from his outburst.

"I believe I told you to leave."

Alvin didn't move. Neither did I. He came up on the balls of his feet then rolled back, flat footed. His anger seemed to abate.

"Why do you push your family away? Can't you talk to us about what you're going through?"

Deciding to try to mend the relationship with my brother, I moved to the lounger and exhaustedly fell into it. "The new man in my life is an FBI agent."

"You know that isn't what I was referring to, but it's a start." He sat down in the chair next to me. "So, you almost married an FBI agent. Care to elaborate?"

"We did have a ceremony but didn't honor the seventy-two-hour waiting period after our license was issued, so our marriage certificate couldn't be filed." That was the bit of information Sticks's lawyer had dug up while we were in New Mexico. No one told me until I was released from the hospital. Not actually being married was a severe blow to my chaste lifestyle choice. That, along with me getting pregnant out-of-wedlock. I was spiraling, and it was taking its toll. I needed to slow my life and get back to meticulously planning.

I reached over and touched Alvin's shoulder. "Thank you for being concerned. I know that you show it through anger." It had only taken me five years of therapy as a teenager for me to come to that conclusion. "I will be more careful from now on. Getting married was impulsive. I can see that now." I stood. "A lot has happened and I'm tired, Alvin. Would you mind leaving, please? And calling off Peter the Wolf, too?"

He stood as well. "I'll leave, but the jury is still out on if I audit your trust fund or not. I need to make sure you're taken care of. That was the one stipulation that Mom and Dad drilled into my head ever since the day you were born." He gave me a hug.

I embraced him, smiling as I pulled away. "I'm sure they wouldn't be disappointed in your concern. Maybe about your approach though. Could you reign in Peter?"

He ruffled my hair. "This is why you're so spoiled, little sis. Everyone gives in to that smile."

Chapter Thirty-One
Necessities

"You're going to need these, Lainee." Marsha was ruining my commitment to pack lighter.

"Three-inch spike heels to a private island get away? I don't think so."

"Sticks could be a shoes salesman again." She wiggled her eyebrows.

I almost caved in but resisted slipping them into my suitcase. "What happened to your advice about being adventurous and not trying the same thing twice?"

"You're going to start listening to my advice on sex now?"

"Not really," I said as I walked to the closet to put the shoes out of Marsha's reach. I knew that if she was given a chance, she would pack them while I wasn't looking. "I was going to modify your plan. I did some research and made a list of what things I'd like to try. So, I think no repetition until round ten is a good rule of thumb."

"Oh, my god, Lainee. You and your rules again."

There was a knock at the open door. Sticks stood, taking up every inch of space in the doorway. "Are you ready for me to take anything? Our Uber is here."

He looked around the room at the three suitcases strewn with clothing and the two accessory bags. "Did I dream the discussion we had about you minimizing your luggage? We're going to an isolated island."

I sighed, knowing he would never understand the logic behind my decision but trudged forward with the explanation anyway. "The trouble with that argument is that the beach is on a private island."

He shook his head. "Already established. Where is this going?"

"Well, that means there are no stores, so if I forget something I need, there is no way to replace it while we're there."

He rubbed his temples. "Let's look at this from a different perspective. We are getting to the island via a Cessna aircraft. Do you want that type of plane to be overloaded with luggage?"

I looked at him, then turned to Marsha. "Help me prioritize."

She took out all of my clothing with the exception of lingerie, bathing suits, and one cover-up. I added three respectable outfits as Sticks dumped my cosmetic tote, digging to find my sunscreen, toothbrush, toothpaste, and hair brush. I managed to slip hair ties, moisturizer, lipstick, mascara, shampoo, conditioner, razor, and lotion into a side pocket before he zipped it, then looked at me. "Shoes?"

Showing him my various pairs of sandals, he said, "Choose two."

Tossing aside my red, turquoise, silver, and pink pairs of sandals, I chose three. I absolutely needed one for each neutral color theme: black, tan, and white.

Sticks walked to the closet and came out with a different pair of heels from the ones Marsha had chosen. These were simplistic, a single strap over the toes with another following up the heel and buckling around the ankle. I may have sighed and briefly reconsidered my New Rule of Ten.

"Looks like you may need help putting these on." Sticks gave me a soft kiss and my body tingled with anticipation. He added, "And purple is my favorite color."

I didn't correct him by telling him they were lavender.

Hilda walked in as we were fighting to get my single bag closed. I gave up and grabbed one accessory bag for the shoes and snuck in a cosmetics case. I was certain that little added weight wouldn't affect the plane.

"The driver needs to leave. He has another ride lined up after yours," Hilda reported.

I followed Sticks out of my room, already feeling naked from leaving so many of my things behind.

***

"I have a confession. I put extra items in the luggage. It might have pushed us over the weight limit. This thing feels like it's coming apart." We had been flying for almost an hour. In an airplane. With a single engine. And no doors. I fought the urge to slip into the brace position but remembered Ronaldo's theories.

"We're going to be fine, Lainee. Just breathe." Sticks was saying through the headset microphone. "Inhale. Two. Three. Four. Exhale. Two. Three. Four."

"There's a reason my family never flew on planes. They were sane. And this is the fifth one I've been on since I've known you. What does that say about you?"

Unperplexed, Sticks smiled and said, "It says I can count. This is actually your sixth plane ride since knowing me."

I counted the flights and squinted my eyes when I realized he was correct if you counted the flight to the main island, then this smaller one. "I'll amend my statement then. This is my fifth destination to be reached by plane since I've known you."

He smiled, and I was distracted from our current dangers until the small aircraft slowed, shifted to the left then resumed its original speed. I gasped. "We can't land, yet. We're going to crash."

He leaned forward to speak with the pilot. "Can you make one more pass before landing?"

The pilot, hearing all of my conversation with Sticks through his linked headphones, shook his head while once again passing the tiny landing strip on the island. "This will have to be the last one. I have to save enough fuel to fly back. Also, I'll have to put the added cost for these passes on your invoice."

Sticks nodded at him. "Understood. Thank you." Then he turned to me. "You're not taking my breathing suggestions seriously, Lainee."

"Well, on a positive note, my anger towards you seems to be helping my fear of landing."

"Your irrational anger. Millions of people choose airplanes as their mode of transportation each day, Lainee."

"You are projecting attitude in your tone, Sticks."

He sighed and pinched the bridge of his nose between his thumb and forefinger. He practiced his own breathing suggestion, then put his arm around me and pointed. "Look at the island. Can you believe this whole thing is ours for three nights?"

The island was full of trees with the exception of the runway along the Southern beach. Along the Eastern side was a bay where the water was bluer, and the sand was whiter than any other place on the island. The only break in the trees were the roofs of two buildings. The larger of the two stood at the border of the bay and wooded area, and the other was a smaller dwelling in the middle of the island adjacent to a small pool of water. There were also two piers, one on either side of the entrance to the bay.

Sticks reached over and stroked my thigh. "We'll have to explore other relaxation techniques to take your mind off the flight before our return trip."

Looking up at the pilot, I was sure he missed the innuendo. He was concentrating on the controls, readying the plane for landing. I was ever thankful that Sticks's need for sex overrode his amygdala's warning that I may be functioning somewhat on the crazy side.

Intertwining our hands, I said, "That's a great

idea. Getting my mind on other things may help. Let's plan what we're going to need to do. How are we getting the luggage to the bungalow? It looks like it's quite a trek. What about food? Has that already been delivered? We don't want to go hungry while we're here, right? What about storage? We'll need to unpack and put everything away. I'll have to see what needs to be organized and inventory supplies once we get there. When was the last time the property was used? How does it get cleaned? Do you think it's dusty? I didn't bring any medications. What if we're allergic to something on the island?"

Sticks physically slumped in his seat. "I don't know if I'll ever recover from this. You just reminded me of Hilda."

Chapter Thirty-Two
Island Time

We were met at the far end of the airstrip by a lanky black man with hair styled in a crew cut. When he smiled, his front tooth gleamed golden off the warm Bahamian sun. "I'm your guide, Tarone Tamblay. I wasn't sure you'd be a landin'."

"Small plane jitters." Sticks said as he put his arm around me. "Are you okay, Lainee?"

"Grateful to be off the plane and on solid ground, that's for sure."

The pilot helped Tarone put our few bags into the bed of the dilapidated compact truck with a look that said he was glad I wasn't on his plane anymore as well. Sticks helped lift me into the cab. Tarone joined us and started the engine. On the third try.

"My wife, Cedella, is at da cabin. She's making sure ev'ry ting be fine for you."

"Do you live on the island? I thought it was deserted." I hadn't envisioned others during our island getaway.

"We only come over when dey be guests. We stay at the shelter up da road and help with food and cleanin' while you be visit'n our paradise." I loved the cadence of his voice, in what I could only imagine was a variant of a Jamaican accent.

Driving down the bumpy and winding dirt road, I wondered which would have been the worse option, sitting in the middle of the cab between the bucket seats on the console or sitting on Sticks's lap. Both came with the danger of no seatbelt. However, sitting in his lap had the disadvantage of Sticks holding my hips to keep me from jostling too much. It was a disadvantage because I remembered how he held my hips as he guided the pace during our vehicular encounter in New Mexico.

The advantage of this seating arrangement was it quickened Sticks's recovery time. I knew from the small circles he was drawing with his thumbs along my lower back, he was already forgetting about my Hilda impersonation. I repositioned myself to sit sideways across his lap and further away from him, toward his knees, hoping to alleviate something that could grow into an awkward situation. Pun intended.

Tarone pointed out the passenger window. "You see dat path? It leads to our place. There's no phone, but we'll leave you a walkie-talkie to get in touch in case you need anyt'ing." The road was now encompassed by mid-level brush on both sides. I could see the bungalow in the distance. There were a few palm trees interspersed on the drive along with flowering trees with a low hanging fruit. My home gardens were impeccably maintained, but even Horacio couldn't have planned a more masterful landscape. As we made it up a small incline, the scene opened, and we could see the ocean behind our lodgings. It was an incredible view.

A woman stood on the wrap around porch of the bungalow. "Welcome to Abacos Cay," she said as we approached. Tarone and Sticks carried in the luggage.

The home was beautiful. Multiple doors stood open to capture the ocean breeze. I walked through the first one. There was a rustic feel and a sense of weightlessness upon entering. Surf boards were stored over the exposed beams in the living area. Instead of traditional seating, the exposed beams also provided support for stretched hammocks. Sticks crawled into one and I had to remind myself that Tarone and Cedella were also in the house or else I might have cuddled up and had my way with him right then. He gave me a sideways grin and I knew he could read my thoughts.

I distracted myself by looking in the kitchen. A full set of pots and pans were organized on a rack hanging from the ceiling and a Keurig coffee machine was on the counter. All of the comforts of home.

Cedella became the tour guide. "The kitchen is fully stocked, and we brought da groceries you requested." Her accent wasn't as pronounced as her husband's. "I start da cooking at six in da evening and it'll be served around six-thirty. Just letting you know so you can plan your activities around that time."

I made a mental note. No sex between 5:45 and 7:00. For three nights. Almost seven hours out of our trip. The disappointment must have shown on my face.

Cedella added, "Of course, if your plans change,

you can always radio to let me know." She winked.

Relieved, I sat in one of the barstools at the counter separating the kitchen from the small dining area furnished with a simple bistro table and two chairs. I sniffed the bouquet of fresh tropical flowers.

"I hope you don't mind fresh cut. Da last lady had allergies. She couldn't take da island and had to leave early. Didn't even wait for us to help her make plans to leave."

I turned to give Sticks an I-told-you-so look.

Sticks didn't notice. He sat up. "You mean Joanna? Tall, leggy, blonde with a scar on her eyebrow?"

Cedella nodded her head.

Sticks's brow furrowed. "I've traveled with her several times and have never known her to have allergies."

"I didn't know you knew her," Cedella said.

I didn't know he knew a Joanna that he traveled with multiple times either.

"Dat woman is so beautiful and sweet. We loved having her stay. Dat man doe." She paused to choose her words carefully. "Dey are not a good match."

"Who is Joanna?" I asked. I knew it was irrational to be jealous. I had questioned my relationship with other men while I was with Sticks. I should have assumed he would have had other women in his life as well. But when you're a short, cute brunette, it is not an ego booster to know your boyfriend's previous travel companion was tall, beautiful, and blonde.

"She's kind of a coworker." Sticks answered

without maintaining eye contact.

I raised an eyebrow.

When he finally looked at me, he said, "Alright. We planned this trip together about a year ago. Everything was paid for, but circumstances changed. The easy solution was her taking the first three days and me taking the last three, with a day off in between so our paths wouldn't overlap when we were with our significant others."

I did a double eyebrow lift.

"Lainee, it was a casual relationship and we split amicably months ago." He stood and walked into the dining area. "At least that's what I thought until she didn't return any of my calls to see how her trip went."

"So, you plan one-week vacations with all your casual relationships? And you were still calling her? Is there anything else I need to know?" I asked.

"Is there anything else you want to know?"

Oh dear, Lord. If that man threw one more of my sayings back at me, I was going to have to have words with him. Which would probably result in him having more sayings to throw back at me. I was just going to have to convince him that they only had the correct meaning when I said them. Instead of mentioning anything in front of company, I gave Sticks a look that let him know he wasn't off the hook.

His grin broadened. His smile was stunning. I was so used to him being the mysterious federal agent who brooded or gave orders. It was nice to see him this relaxed. I got caught up in his mood and returned his smile. Until I remembered I was mad at him.

Tarone cleared his throat. "Cedella, why don't you unpack for dem while I tell dem about the island?"

I relaxed a little at the thought of being pampered and listened to information about how to contact them and about the various features and trails of the island. Fifteen minutes later, the couple left.

"Before you say anything, Lainee, I got you a gift."

We walked into the bedroom and there was a cellophane wrapped basket in the middle of the bed and a bottle of champagne chilling on the bedside table.

"That was sweet, but I didn't get you anything."

"It's fine. I plan on benefitting from your gifts." He said as he pulled me toward the bed.

Chapter Thirty-Three
Count 'em Up

Sitting atop a blanket on the beach while the sun rose on our last morning on the island, the ocean lulled me into a state of Nirvana. I missed the sounds of Sticks approaching and was startled when he sat behind me, his legs straddling me. He gave me a reassuring pat as I leaned into him, my back touching his chest. We sat for minutes in awe of the view. I wanted to preserve every precious moment I had left with him.

"It's beautiful here," I said.

"Almost as beautiful as you, Lainee." He gathered my hair that the ocean breeze occasionally whipped in his face, twisted it, and placed it over my shoulder. "It's almost magical." He began kissing my neck but abruptly stopped. "Before we get distracted again, I need to tell you what's been happening. I haven't found an opportunity to bring this up yet, and we're running out of time."

I shifted slightly to look at him, holding my breath, waiting for the words I didn't want to come. I knew he would be moving on.

"As you know, I spent the last two weeks in Arizona, trying to get Caitlynn settled. Now that Brad's being charged, it looks like there is going to be a three-way custody battle between both sets of grandparents and me."

"As the biological father, wouldn't you have more of an advantage?"

"Not necessarily. You have to remember, regardless of the circumstances, I haven't been in her life. Added to that, I just got off administrative leave from the FBI for disobeying the direct order from the regional director. Their attorneys could use that against me."

"I didn't know you were on leave."

"It was merely a slap on the wrist for leaving with you when I was told to stay on the case. No need to worry." He reached for a strand of my hair that had escaped, twisting it around his finger, lost in thought. "I made the decision to leave the Bureau."

"But you love your job, Sticks."

"I loved my job because that was all I had. Now, I have Caitlynn. I'm using the remainder of my vacation time getting settled in Tucson and turning in my notice when I get back. I've applied for the Pima County Assistant Deputy ME position and have a second-round interview this upcoming week. With my FBI connections and medical background, I have a decent shot." He gently caressed my arm. "But what I really wanted to talk about was where this leaves you and me."

My whole body felt hollow. I had picked up on the hint that he only listed Caitlynn as a person he had in his life. I was going to give him an easy out. "You don't have to worry about me. Concentrate on

Caitlynn. She just lost her mother, the man she thought was her father is indirectly responsible for the death, and instead of finding peace at home, people are fighting over her."

"You gave me a lot to think about with Caitlynn in one sentence. How much should I be a part of uprooting her world?" He paused for a moment. "I need to give that more thought than I can devote to it right now. We need to talk about us." He looked into my eyes. "You matter to me."

That was an unexpected turn in our conversation. I had anticipated a dismissal.

"I'm going to be busy rebooting my career along with establishing a relationship with my daughter. Not to mention, I'll be tied up with the legal aspect of the custody fight. Those are big changes to contend with in a short period of time. I don't know how much I'll be able to see you with us being so far apart, but I don't want you out of my life. This would be so much easier if we lived in the same state."

My brother's words rushed through my head. *You get to sit around the pool with your friends and pretend to play house with whichever guy comes along.* I had to start taking my relationships more seriously, but should a long-distance relationship be the one I committed to?

"Sticks, we agreed rushing to get married was a mistake and that we need to take things slowly to get to know each other. Picking up my life and running to Arizona doesn't fit into that agreement." I shifted to face him more, placing my hands on his impressively broad chest. A tingle went through me. "Plus, what would your mother say?"

"I don't want to talk about my mother right now." Sticks closed the distance between us.

His kiss was soft, so tender I wanted to cry. We were going to end our adventure by ending our relationship. It didn't matter that he still wanted to be with me. Logistics were against it.

His hands began exploring my body. I could feel their roughness as they trailed along my shoulders, down my back, finally coming to rest on my hips.

When I shifted to sit astride him, the kisses became demanding and insistent. Sticks began pulling at the strings on my bikini top, urgent to uncover its treasure. Frustrated, he asked, "How many strings are on this thing?" He had pulled all of them together, making the knot tighter. I swatted his hands away as I reached around to untie it. His hands immediately covered what my top exposed, kneading and massaging, with an occasional twist. His fingers eventually trailed south and found another purpose, while his mouth took over their previous assignment.

I slid my hand under the waistband of his swimsuit. Sticks was disappointed when I stopped at the hidden pocket inside instead of venturing further down. I got out one of the condoms.

"I can't believe you only brought twelve." I said as I tore the package then bent to creatively put it on.

"It was either that or thirty-six. For three nights. I didn't want to be presumptuous." He ran his fingers through my hair, guiding my creative efforts.

"Besides, I like the options it opened."

When it was in place, he flipped me over, lifting me onto my hands and knees, and positioned himself behind me.

As much as I wanted to move forward, or more specifically backward in this case, I found my voice. "Wait! We can't do this one yet."

I heard him sigh as he sat down on the towel. Frustrated, Sticks said, "Go ahead. Count them up."

"Okay, first was 'ride 'em cowboy' on our New Mexico adventure and second was 'the mission statement.'" I said as I put my bathing suit back in place.

He impatiently ticked off the rest. "Third was 'under the sea.' Fourth, 'the dog and pony show.' After that were five and six, the 'side by side,' and the 'I wanna rock.' Which brings us to seven, the 'Swedish bike ride.'" He smiled wickedly. "That was an interesting surprise at the lookout."

"Yes, but I don't think it should count since I couldn't follow through with it." I made a mental note not to attempt any more of Marsha's suggestions. "So, depending on how we total them, we still have to engage in three or four more activities before we try this one again. Unless…" I tapped my finger on my mouth a few times. "Do you think we should count the 'side shows'?" The surprises in the gift basket Sticks brought had been inspirational for alternate spontaneous acts.

"God, Lainee, your plan of wanting to be adventurous is having the opposite effect." Sticks laid back, packed his deflating happiness into his shorts, and bent his elbow over his eyes. "We need to put all of the rules on hold."

I knew he was getting upset, and I wanted to let go and be free. However, I needed to rein in my impulses. My behavior had been out of control for the last six months, resulting in near disasters. Plus, I knew this relationship was not moving forward. We would have the next few hours, then it would be over. I couldn't separate my emotions from my actions any longer. I was getting caught up in the fairy tale and needed to return to reality.

After a moment, he sat up and crawled closer to embrace me. "Can you trust me enough to let go of your lists?"

"What do you mean?" My heart began pounding. There was no way he could know. I had never even told Marsha. But something in his tone made it clear he had found out. I tried to push away from him.

His embrace tightened. "I know why you make lists. I know what happened, Lainee." He kissed the top of my head. "When you were four."

I tried to pull away again. I felt dizzy. My hands were tingling, and I couldn't catch my breath. I knew the signs. I was having a panic attack.

Sticks cradled me. "How your grandfather died."

A tear ran down my cheek as he stroked my hair. "It wasn't your fault, Lainee."

"You're wrong, Sticks. They've all been my fault."

Chapter Thirty-Four
The Blame Game

I knew what the doctors said. A panic attack was simply an adrenaline rush. If you did nothing, it would be over in ten minutes after the adrenaline left your body. The doctors were wrong. I could never remain still. It made me feel better to do something. I got up and began walking to the bungalow.

Sticks followed. "Lainee, we really need to talk about this."

I ignored him.

"It's affected you almost your entire life. It will get better if you don't run from it."

"How did you even find out? No one is supposed to know."

"I read your file."

I stopped, keeping my back to him, suddenly feeling drained. He had told me before. Had given hints that he knew more about me than I had told him. He was reassuring about my financial portfolio when I was worried about my siblings being critical of my expenses. He tried to lower my grandmother off her pedestal when he broke her lamp. He even knew about the flapper costume that I only wore for a sorority promotional event. I never imagined how detailed the information in an FBI dossier would be.

"You should have respected my privacy."

"When I read it, you were simply someone who was rescued by my team. I never dreamed it would be about the person I'm falling in love with."

Slowly turning, I asked, "What did you say?"

"You heard me correctly. God, it goes against everything I've always stood for to move this fast in a relationship. I feel like I have to fight for control every time I'm around you." He put his hands on my shoulders, then trailed soft caresses down my arms. "I want to blurt out how beautiful you are, how you brighten every room, the intriguing way your mind works, how your compassion is inspiring. And, yes, how much I love you."

I stood silent and motionless.

He asked, "Scared you off, did I?"

"I'm processing," I answered.

He needed me to respond, but the silence grew. Finally, I said, "I don't deserve it. I don't accept it."

"I love you whether you accept it or not."

"I have to get ready to go home." Mentally, I tallied each item I needed to pack as I walked away.

"Lainee, please don't walk away from me."

When we got to the lanai of our bungalow, I turned toward him. "I can't let you in, Sticks. I can't let anyone in. Everyone I love dies or gets hurt, and it's always my fault."

"This is what we have to talk about. These things aren't your fault."

I knew he was only trying to help, but he had been

misinformed. "Yes, they are. If I hadn't gone into the lake when I wasn't supposed to, my grandfather never would have had a heart attack trying to rescue me."

"I'm a medical doctor. Your grandfather died because he smoked for years, had a horrendous diet, and went against his doctor's advice after his first two heart attacks."

"His first two?"

"Yes. It was his third heart attack that killed him. No, strike that. It was the choices he made throughout his life that killed him. A four-year-old girl cannot hold herself responsible for decades over something she had no control over."

"No, I went swimming when I wasn't supposed to. I woke up early from my nap. I was scheduled to swim with my grandparents at four o'clock. I shouldn't have gone in at two-thirty."

"Your grandmother and grandfather were arguing by the pool when they heard you screaming. He had been caught cheating with the maid in the pool house."

"No, my grandfather loved my grandmother. She was the love of his life. Grandma Elaine always told me how they met in a ballroom and they danced the entire evening."

"Your grandfather was in a band. Your grandparents met in a barroom, and the dancing they did that night was the horizontal tango. They had to get married, Lainee."

This couldn't be true. My grandmother had told me grand tales of their courtship. "You're wrong." I tried to live my life like she told me she had led hers.

Were all of her Southern belle traditions and guidelines a lie?

"It's a lot to take in, Lainee, but it's true. I know you started planning out every part of your day after your grandfather died and adhered to a strict schedule. You were treated for obsessive compulsive disorder because of it."

"That was in my file, too? I was a child. Aren't those records sealed?"

"The details from the doctor are sealed but insurance claims are easier to access. Those came up when we did the intensive background check. Remember, you showed up out of nowhere on a major criminal investigation. We needed to know why."

"Well, I recovered from all of that."

"You stopped following a rigid schedule and your compulsive repetitions but replaced those behaviors with making detailed lists. Hilda was worried that you'd regress after your parents died, but once you began being active again, you became overly impulsive instead." He stepped forward and cupped his hand around my neck and caressed my chin with his thumb. "They didn't die because of you, Lainee. You have to trust me on this. There is no amount of planning that stops death."

"I know. I went to see my grandmother, just like I did every week, except this time I had congestion. I must have given Grandma Elaine a cold that turned into pneumonia. She got sick and died before my next scheduled visit."

"Your grandmother was immobile and pulmonary

secretions built up in her lungs causing pneumonia. It was not your fault, Lainee."

"My parents blamed me, too. They stopped talking to me after my grandmother's death."

"People change patterns after their loved ones die. It is a normal process. They were grieving."

"And my parents died because they didn't want to interrupt my schedule. They said I should stay in and finish taking down the Christmas decorations like I had planned to do."

"You were doing something no one else wants to do. They were probably happy to let you complete it."

"I stopped meticulously planning after that, and when I made lists again, bad things started happening. But mostly to me, so it's better."

"From my viewpoint, that's worse. I want you safe, but I also want you to stop being so hard on yourself. We need to enjoy the time we have left together. Can we try to do that?"

I nodded. He grabbed my hand and headed to the beach. He let go and ran ahead of me, drawing something in the sand with his foot.

As I approached, I could see he had written *Sticks and Lainee*.

"How sweet! I want to get a picture." I reached into my beach bag to pull out my phone. A wave came and washed his message away before I could get a photo. It reminded me of how everything was fleeting. "It's all so temporary, Sticks."

"This was not a calling card from the universe. It happens. Don't make more of this than it is. I just told you I loved you. As hard as it was not hearing the same thing from you, I don't think we are temporary. I think this is just the beginning. Are you going to let disappearing words in the sand make your decision?"

"No, I'm not, and I'm sorry I can't say the words to you right now. I'm going to need time."

"All I needed to hear was that you were going to give us a chance." He kissed me. "Now, that we've had this discussion, I think we need to rewrite our mission statement." He easily untied my top this time, letting it be carried by the wind before falling to the sand a few feet away.

I stepped back and posed, watching while Sticks's gaze devoured me. I could feel my nipples tighten in the cool breeze and saw his pupils dilate. I loved having this effect on him. Taking the lead, I walked to him and wrapped my arms around his neck. Our lips collided. The kiss exploded, and I wound my legs around his waist.

Sticks moved to the blanket and laid me gently upon it. He traced my lips with his finger then my collarbone, and down to the fullness of my breast. His actions were deliberate. I could tell he was forcing himself to move slowly. His breath was shallow as he dipped his head to my navel. He brushed off the sand and kissed my stomach. I ran my fingers through his hair and moved my legs to either side of his head. Raising my hips, I untied my bottoms at the sides, offering him a much better feast. He stuck with the appetizers, though, making sure no part of my abdomen or inner thighs were left unkissed.

I pulled at his hair and moaned, "Please."

He lifted his head and sat up. "Not yet."

I was bereft, pulling him to me and moving against him. He stilled, not allowing me to rush him.

"This is the first time we are going to make love. We're going to do it slowly. I love you, Lainee."

Chapter Thirty-Five
Lectures

After making several revisions to the mission statement, we petted the 'lazy dog' and cut it up using 'scissors.' All of which were why I was packing my clothes by rolling them up instead of using my usual KonMori organizational strategies. I looked over my checklist, trying to remember if I had everything.

Sticks opened the screened door, holding up the walkie-talkie. "Tarone and Cedella still aren't answering. I've walked around to get a better signal and tried different channels."

"That's unusual. They're typically very responsive. Let them have a break, I'll write a thank you note before we leave," I said as I mentally put one more thing on my to do list.

He walked into the bedroom. "Are you still packing? Just put everything you see that's yours in the suitcase. Hilda can help sort it out when we get home. She likes taking care of you."

I lifted the lingerie set he had given me. "Do you want Hilda to help me with everything?" I also grabbed the love oils and lotions, which were also part of my surprise package from Sticks.

"Maybe we should take care of some things

ourselves." He conceded. Reaching for me then pulling me close, he kissed me.

I enjoyed the attention but pulled away when he started reaching for areas down south. "I hate to stop, but we need to stay on schedule."

He stuffed all my clothes into my bag, zipped it up, then carried it to the front door next to his. "I asked Tarone to make arrangements for a boat to take us to the main island since you had a hard time with the chartered airplane. He said to be ready by two o'clock at the western dock, but I didn't get a confirmation."

"He was dependable. I'm sure he put it all in place." I decided to follow Sticks's lead and walked into the bathroom to do a broad sweep of my cosmetics and toiletries, cringing when I realized that I didn't check the lids to the containers. They could leak their contents at any moment. Just in case, I stuffed the tote with tissues to protect the bottles as well as to soak up any possible spills. I took a deep breath. Now I was ready to be spontaneous.

Sticks met me in the bathroom doorway. "My girlfriend did something unplanned. We are making progress." Call me juvenile, but I felt a tingle when he called me his girlfriend.

"You act like organizing a marriage ceremony in one day and having relations in the car were meticulously planned events."

"This may sound odd but doing something as mundane as throwing things in a cosmetic case makes it seem more significant."

"Well, I'm not planning on making this a habit."

He imitated my Southern accent. "Since the definition of spontaneous is not planning," He switched to his own voice. "I'd say we're on the right track." Sticks leaned over and kissed me. I wrapped my arms around his neck and his hands traced my spine, then he cupped and kneaded my posterior once again.

I broke the kiss and pushed him onto the bed. "It's a good thing I'm already packed. We have a few minutes to spare."

***

Thankfully, it took us a more than a few minutes to complete our activity. Unfortunately, we were now having to hustle to get to the dock.

Sticks was buttoning his Hawaiian shirt, covering his glorious broad chest. "Let's try to get down there before I'm charged a late fee. I can only imagine how much the pilot tacked on to our flight bill for our trip over here, and I'm about to be unemployed."

He gathered my oversized suitcase along with his and walked out onto the lanai. I followed with the cosmetics bag. We could see the boat approaching in the distance and set off across the muddy yard then the beach, the rolling suitcases becoming burdensome in the sand.

"Here, I'll get one of the suitcases." I took the handle of the smallest one. It didn't budge. Sticks's grip was tighter.

"I've got it, Lainee. Don't worry. I wouldn't want

you to think I'm not being a gentleman. After all, I've got a three-hour trip with you before hitting the main island and I'd rather not have to endure a lecture."

"I don't give lectures," I said. "I simply have conversations that include reprimands and offer valuable lessons."

He caught my arm and pulled me closer, giving me a peck on the cheek. "That gave me an idea for the perfect Christmas gift for you. A pocket dictionary, just so you can look up words and prove my point."

"That does it. Now you're getting a lesson about the subtle nuances of the language of Lainee." This time I kissed him, wishing the accessory bag slung around my neck wasn't a barrier between us as he deepened the kiss.

We heard the boat begin blowing its horn, which was not necessary. It hadn't even reached the dock yet. The blaring kept penetrating the sounds of the waves crashing onto the shore. Finally, we broke apart and looked at the approaching vessel.

There were at least three men on deck. One held a long pole, the other two were reaching over the side, hauling something onboard from the water.

"Is that...?" My question trailed off as I looked over at Sticks.

He had already unzipped the front pocket of his suitcase and pulled out a satellite phone. "Lainee, go to the bungalow and call the only number stored in this phone. Tell them my name, where we are, that we have a 10-54, and I'm needing assistance."

"What can they do? This isn't American soil, is

it?"

"Lainee, please just do as I asked. We are on a deserted island and there is possibly a dead body. You need to get off the beach now."

I almost blurted out that, technically, he hadn't asked me anything, only told me what to do, but I didn't think he would appreciate spontaneity in this case. Instead, I ran to the bungalow, calling the number immediately.

A man answered abruptly on the other end. "Yes."

"Is this the FBI?" I asked.

Silence.

"Are you still there?"

"Yes." He answered as gruff as before.

"I'm calling for Agent Torres."

More silence.

I decided to do exactly as Sticks told me. "I'm with Agent Clint Torres on Abacos Cay Island in the Bahamas. There is a 10-54, and he needs back up."

"And?" The man asked.

"And you need to learn how to speak with manners. Using more than one syllable words and more than one word per sentence."

"You must be Lainee," he said before disconnecting.

It was disturbing that a stranger knew who I was but refreshing that he decided to take my advice.

***

I heard the approaching footsteps. As I held the

canister of non-stick cooking spray in one hand and one of the stiletto heels Sticks had chosen in the other, I prepared to defend myself. The steps were closer, now on the lanai. I mentally retraced my actions after my call to the mysterious stranger. I had gone through the bungalow closing and locking all doors and windows. That helped me feel secure. Whoever was out there would have to get through a locked door first.

The handle jiggled. Then a voice called out. "It's me, Lainee, open up." Thank, God! It was Sticks.

I stood to go to the door, but it crashed open before I could take a step. So much for security measure one.

And security measure two. I had spread my tubes of lipstick, mascara, eyeliner, spice containers, and anything else cylindrical I could find to use as a booby trap at the most likely point of entry. If this had been a Hollywood movie, the perpetrator would have rushed into the area and lost his balance sliding over the items, giving the victim valuable time to escape. In reality, everything rolled out of the way when the door swept it aside as it opened.

A huge guy dressed in black came in before Sticks.

"Mac, calm down." Sticks said as he kicked aside the few remaining security devices and looked at the shoes I had lined up in a semi-circle around me to throw as needed. For back up, I had my perfume and the heat protectant spray for my hair within easy reach. "What is all of this?" Sticks asked, a smile spreading across his face.

"It's my defense plan. I wanted to be prepared for whatever walked through the door." It might not have been much, but it had given me something to do while waiting, plus it had provided a modicum sense of security.

Sticks pulled me to him and kissed the top of my head. "You're always surprising me." He tucked me at his side. "This is Mac. He's an old friend and on the team to help us."

"Nice to meet you," I said as I held out my hand.

He merely nodded his head.

Trying not to take offense, I discreetly put my hand to my side. "You're part of the team? Where is everyone else?"

"I was already on my way before the official call went out. The others are still hashing out protocols and procedures."

"Well, thanks for coming. I'm glad we're not alone."

I didn't realize how untrue those words would become.

Chapter Thirty-Six
Alternative Defense Plans

It was sweltering in the bungalow. When barricading myself in, I had lost the only cooling factor, the breeze. As the men went through the area opening doors and windows, I quietly went to the bathroom and looked in the mirror. Oh, dear. I couldn't believe I had been introduced to someone while looking so disheveled. There was no possible way I could rationalize this look as the more Southern acceptable description of dewy from perspiration. I was downright sweaty. My hair was stuck to random places on my forehead and neck. I cringed when remembering Sticks had kissed my hair. Then there were the large stains on my shirt under my armpits and along my lower back. The most positive thought I could come up with is that my skin had a radiant sheen to it. That was probably a stretch, but it's what I was clinging to.

I took a quick shower to cool down but was left with a dilemma. My suitcase with alternate clothing options was still on the pier. I chose to rinse then wring out the t-shirt and put it on wet. It would work. I couldn't tell what was sweat or water and the see-through aspect of a wet t-shirt was minimized by my pastel floral bra. Maybe the men would think it was a bathing suit. I put my hair in a ponytail and decided that was the best it was going to get.

I walked into the dining area.

"Do you feel better now?" Sticks stood to hug me and pointed to my cosmetics bag on the counter. "I think I got everything packed away again."

"Yes, I do, and thank you."

Sticks pulled me into his lap as he sat at the small dining table across from Mac.

"It's been an eventful day. Who did they pull from the water? Was it Cedella or Tarone?" I asked.

"No, it was Joanna." Sticks's jaw set and he swallowed hard. "The Tamblays have not been located."

"Do you think they're victims or suspects?"

"We have no evidence either way. There's no sign of a struggle at their hut, and we can't rule out they didn't flee. There are only minimal supplies and clothing, but they were only planning to be here a week, so that wouldn't be unusual. We shouldn't make any assumptions, but my gut tells me they weren't involved."

Mac spoke, "As far as suspects go, you two can't be ruled out."

"What?" I asked. "That's ridiculous, Sticks is an FBI agent."

"Lainee, he's right. Any law enforcement officer is going to be suspicious of anyone on this island. I can't be sure of time of death, but it didn't appear she had been in the water very long. Ocean life is not kind to bodies and most of hers was still intact." I grimaced, and he took both of my hands in his. "The men from the boat are taking her to the morgue on the main island. I tried to get them to wait for you, but they were spooked and said the police could figure out who could leave."

"I wouldn't have left you alone, Sticks." I gave him a quick kiss before turning to Mac. "How did you get here?"

"I got a voicemail from Torres saying Joanna left the island early and asking me to look into it. Once I got his message, I made a few calls and found out she hadn't reported in. Then I couldn't get in touch with Torres, so I came right away." He was perfectly still as he spoke. Nothing moved but his lips. It was eerie.

"You came here without getting any facts?" I asked.

"The only fact I needed to know was that Torres thought something was off. He and Joanna know how to take care of themselves. If they needed backup, I was expecting trouble." He finally moved, leaning onto the table. "What I wasn't expecting, was you."

I was taken aback by Mac's abrasiveness but didn't want him to think I was intimidated. I leaned on the table as well and said, "Surprise."

The tension in the room increased. Sticks shifted, turning me slightly away from Mac, and said, "We'll have a few hours before anyone will come. Let's use this time to our advantage. When the investigators get here, they're going to know Joanna was my former lover. Their first line of thought will be either Lainee or I killed her out of jealousy."

"Except she had left the island before we arrived. Neither of us had seen her. I didn't even know she existed until Cedella mentioned her."

"We can tell them that, but they aren't going to believe it until Cedella confirms it. And she can't do that if she can't be found." Sticks turned to Mac. "Something Cedella said has been bothering me. You'd gone on missions with Joanna and were still assigned with her. Had she been having medical issues? Allergies? Anything like that?"

"None that she told me about."

Sticks nodded. "Did you know who she was seeing?"

"Word was she was still hung up on you." He looked at me, eyes glinting. "Looks like you had no problem moving on."

My instinct was to move closer to Sticks, but I forced myself to stand and go into the kitchen. Mac was making me nervous. There was a dangerous undercurrent. I wanted Sticks to have full range of motion if needed to defend us. If Sticks was feeling threatened, he didn't show it.

I opened the refrigerator, gathering the grape tomatoes, bell peppers, zucchini, and jar of olives. "There are still some supplies in here. Should I try to throw something together to eat?" I also grabbed the spiral noodles and olive oil from the pantry.

Sticks said, "Yes. Sounds great. Thanks." Then to Mac, he said, "Joanna never gave me the impression she had any lingering feelings. In fact, she was the one who broke it off."

"Because you never moved forward and always kept your distance. You had to know she was more invested in the relationship than you were."

Sticks thought about Mac's words. "Mac, I had no idea. You know as well as I do that Joanna was an elite agent. If she didn't want me to know, I wasn't going to find out. Sounds like she was sharing more with you than with me."

I put on water to boil for the pasta and found the garlic powder that had not helped deter anyone from entering the bungalow earlier. I knelt down, getting a knife from where I had hidden them earlier. It might sound crazy, but I felt that if I was close enough to use a knife on someone, that person was close enough to disarm me and use it against me. I had decided to hide the knives instead, so no one would be able to access them. Cooking spray, perfume, and hair products seemed to be the better choice with a longer range if I was in a combat situation.

I looked over at the men. They were statues, both assessing one another. I got the feeling Sticks had now picked up on Mac's dangerous vibes.

Chapter Thirty-Seven
Mindful Meditations

This started as a great idea for a distraction but cooking for Sticks for the first time quickly lost its luster under the pressure of such a hostile environment. As I cut the vegetables, I imagined me having to protect myself with a knife. Slicing tomato and zucchini were one thing, but could I slice through flesh if I needed to? Then there was the disadvantage of not having a recipe. I thought this was the dish Cedella had described the previous day, but felt it was missing something.

I moved to the walkie-talkie charging nearby and hoped against all hope that Cedella would be available to walk me through cooking the meal. Maybe they couldn't be reached earlier because they had gone to get supplies. I pressed the button and a static-y screeching noise came from Mac's camo jacket flung over the kitchen counter. It was feedback from the walkie-talkies being so close together.

"What the hell are you doing?" Mac yelled, rising so fast that the metal bistro chair fell backward, crashing onto the floor. My heart was pounding in my chest. I placed my fingertips of one hand on the edge of the counter, needing the slight support and raised my other to cover my mouth. If he had the Tamblays' walkie-talkie, what had he done to them?

"The better question is, what the hell did you do, Mac?" Sticks's voice was calm, distracting Mac's attention away from me. "Why don't you tell me what happened? Maybe we can find a solution without any more bloodshed. What happened between you and Joanna?"

"We got into an argument. Nothing big, but she said she wanted to end it." He ran his hand down his face and pulled at his rough beard. "When she took a shower, I looked at her phone to see if there was someone else and found the messages from you. About how you couldn't wait to be on the island. I thought she was shipping me off to make room for you." Mac began pacing. "I didn't mean for anything to happen. I was just mad. Went in the bathroom and threw back the shower curtain." His voice revealed his despair despite his face remaining expressionless. "She just slipped. That was all. She turned to face me and slipped."

"Oh, my god, Sticks. We had sex in that shower," I said, then regretted it, not only because I had been indiscreet but also because Mac's focus had been on Sticks. That was no longer the case. Before, Mac had dismissed me because he hadn't seen me as a threat. Now, he saw me standing with a knife.

Sticks was deliberate as he walked to the entrance of the kitchen, placing himself between Mac and me.

Cornered in the kitchen, I willed my feet to move, but they were hesitant to follow my directions.

Instead, I placed the knife on the counter and stated to Mac, "So, it was an accident and you panicked. I'm sure the authorities will understand."

Mac's eyes narrowed. "I don't panic. I did exactly what needed to be done." He told of how he hid Joanna behind the Tamblays' hut where they have cool storage for supplies, wrote a note explaining why he and Joanna had to leave the island, and was going to wait until everyone left to dispose of the body. "It would have worked if the man wouldn't have started clearing out everything."

"Where are the Tamblays?" Sticks asked.

"A golden boy like you should be able to figure it out, Torres." Mac looked at Sticks with contempt. "You, with your off-the-chart IQ. Everything you've done is perfect—physical training, top-notch marksmanship, combat simulations. Every goddamned thing, you excelled at. You'd rise up the ranks, get your promotions, then feel lost without me, your little sidekick, your childhood friend being left behind." Mac scoffed. "'*Don't worry*', you'd say, '*I'll talk to them. If they want me, they'll take you.*' Like I was the imperfection they would have to accept if the powers that be wanted your perfection."

"It wasn't like that, Mac. I was honoring the pact we made as kids."

"Well, I grew up and left childish things behind. I was breaking free of you with Joanna. She was going to be all mine."

"I was never in a competition with you."

"No, you never felt I was good enough to compete

with you." Mac's voice got louder. He was becoming more agitated. "You sure left me behind in Afghanistan. The FBI came calling and you couldn't wait to be whisked away. Finally, you didn't have much pull. Took months for you to get me on as a field agent. Surely with all of your training as an elite agent, you can figure out what happened to a couple of island caretakers."

Sticks took a step forward, giving me more space to escape. I still couldn't move. I hadn't known any of this about him. Looking back, every honor, trophy, and photo of him displayed at his childhood home ended after he graduated. I thought he had peaked in high school. I had just found out that was only the beginning of his feats. He was probably more dangerous than I had ever imagined.

"You know what happened to them." Mac continued, "I followed the training manual we live by and tied up all loose ends." Mac was back to ignoring me. He and Sticks stood staring at one another. "Now you and the little lady have become loose ends." Mac lunged as Sticks stepped to the side then plowed into Mac, sending them both crashing into the wall.

Sticks yelled, "Lainee, go now." He had somehow managed to get Mac into a headlock.

I didn't want to leave Sticks but realized that if I stayed, he would have to protect both of us. He would have more of an advantage if I couldn't be used as leverage. "I'll be at the Swedish spot," I said, knowing he would know that meant where we hiked the day before.

I wondered exactly what type of training Sticks had received. I remembered the hard, edgy exterior he projected when I first met him. Actually, it wasn't that hard to imagine. Currently, power and danger were exuding from every pore of his body. Still holding the knife, I ran to the door and wondered, *who have I gotten mixed up with?*

My gaze turned to Mac. I stared him down as I left. I was sure he would have been intimidated had he seen it and not been struggling to get out of Sticks's headlock at the time.

***

I found the hiking trail Sticks and I had used the previous day. At first, I tried to make sure I was covering my tracks but found that doesn't work as well in real life as it does in the movies. I left more evidence in the form of trampled brush by trying to sweep away any impressions I might have made in the first place. Not to mention the creepy-crawlies I displaced, who thanked me by jumping or flying at me. Then there were the poor souls that I accidentally stepped on. The crunching sound made as they were squashed under my soon-to-be-thrown-away bedazzled flip flops seemed to echo as I pressed on through the foliage to the rendezvous point. I was rather proud of myself for being able to handle the wilderness on my own.

I heard noises in the distance behind me and Sticks yelled, "Lainee, hide."

I made my way off the path and heard Sticks shout again, this time from farther away "Lainee, I said to take cover." He was a brilliant man, leading Mac away from me while alluding that I was in the same area. If something happened to Sticks, Mac would be looking for me in the wrong place. Although, I felt it wouldn't hurt if I was further off the path.

Counting my steps and stopping at every twenty, I quickly marked trees with the knife. I did it on the side of the tree opposite the direction I was traveling. If anyone was following me, the prints wouldn't be seen by them, but if I needed to find my way back to the trail, I would have no problem finding my symbols.

Once I felt I had gone far enough into the dense underbrush, I saw a large rock and ducked behind it. For once, I couldn't think of a damn thing I needed to put on a to do list. My usual ability to disassociate myself from a problem had deserted me. Remembering the calming meditation techniques I had learned recently, I sat in the full lotus position and, straightening my spine to elongate my body, tried to create an atmosphere of mindfulness.

First, I targeted the breath, imagining the flow as it replenished the cells in my body. Next came cleansing my mind of all thought. Not easy to do when you were being hunted, so I moved on to the following phase, concentrating on the here and now. Again, a dead end—hopefully not literally—because being in the here and now wasn't really my ideal setting.

Lastly, I focused on senses other than sight. What

was I feeling? Hearing? Smelling? This was the easiest to accomplish. I quickly ran through the sensations; the way the damp ground felt under me, the itchiness at my ankle, the fly I felt on my upper left arm, a gentle breeze rustling through my hair. Breathing some more, I targeted what I was hearing. I could hear the sound of the ocean, birds in the trees, and the drone of frenzied buzzing to my right. Then the smell struck me. It was slight at first but once I noticed it, there was no mistaking what was wafting my way. Halting my meditation, I opened my eyes.

And looked.

About twenty yards away, I could see the insects buzzing over fallen banana plant leaves. Under them, I saw three exposed, bare feet. I slowly walked over and lifted one of the large leaves. It was Tarone Tamblay. He definitely had a gunshot wound in his forehead and what looked to be two in his chest. I removed two more leaves, and confirmed the other body was Cedella. She had the same wounds as her husband. From my true crime shows, I had learned that when people were killed in this manner, the murderer was trained.

I knew that Mac had murdered them, but it made me wonder about Sticks. He and Mac were co-workers. Yes, I knew Sticks was an FBI agent, but I also knew that he covered up the fact that Cade had shot my captor during my first case. The local police determined that it had been Paulo Bellagio and none of the agents on site the day of my rescue contradicted this assumption. I was very thankful at the time that

Cade would not be prosecuted for murder, because even though it had been self-defense, sometimes it was difficult to prove. I looked up to Sticks at the time because I felt he was protecting Cade from the wrath of the Bellagios. Now, I was seeing it as obstruction of justice. Then there was Mac's statement about Sticks excelling at his training and how he and Joanna were able to take care of themselves. What had Sticks done in his past?

Chapter Thirty-Eight
Third Time's the Charm

My mind wouldn't focus. I vacillated between thoughts of the Tamblays' last moments of life, to the possibility of the same outcome for me, and finally to what would happen if I survived. All of this had changed my perception of Sticks.

My body, however, was on a single course. Its message was loud and clear. Walking a stretch away, I emptied the contents of my stomach and, after a brief rest, I felt much more in control.

I stood and was temporarily disoriented by the overgrowth. I made my way back to the rock I had hid behind and counted my paces until I found my first mark. Following it and the others, I made it to the trail.

I turned toward the bungalow, abandoning my plans to go to the lookout point and listened for any signs of the men approaching. I held the knife down at my side. I didn't want to fall in the uneven terrain and accidentally impale myself, which would seem like an obscure thought until one factored in that I had actually seen that happen to someone on my previous case.

Dear goodness, what had become of my life? I began to count how many dead bodies I had seen in the last six months. It says a lot about my recent lifestyle choices when I hadn't gotten the final total before making it back to the clearing for the bungalow. But that might have been because I was also thinking about what else could kill me if I was stranded on this island. Malaria and Cholera were just a few of the causes I came up with as I swatted at a mosquito and wished I had something to drink.

Upon entering the bungalow, I could tell there had been a struggle inside. Items and furnishings were strewn throughout the living and dining areas. In addition, there was a trail of blood leading to the French doors. I sent up a silent prayer. *Please let it be Mac's.*

After grabbing bottled water and applying extra-strength bug repellant, I put both, along with the knife, in a small knapsack left by a previous guest and strategized my next actions. Both men had trained for combat in adverse conditions. I had little chance of overpowering Mac or helping Sticks. I had studied the map of the island and knew the South trail led to the landing strip. That would be the most likely way the other members of the rescue team would arrive. If I could make it there, I could get help. Plan in place, I exited the back doors.

After walking what seemed hours, but in reality was no longer than thirty minutes, I became more confident. Blocking out the images of the Tamblays lying together in a bloodied heap, I instead planned self-defense moves. I would not be an easy mark.

Mac suddenly stepped onto the path in front of

me. "This is a pleasant surprise. I lost your boyfriend, but you are going to be much more fun. Not as challenging, but more fun."

I turned to escape, but he caught me by my hair. Running through my list of survival moves from earlier in my walk, I fought my instinct to pull away. Instead, I reached up and grabbed his hand, pulling it into my scalp. In the online video I watched, this should be painful to his knuckles and cause his grip to release.

Instead, he laughed. "Someone is putting her training to good use." He leaned in and whispered into my ear. "Too bad it won't work on me."

With him being so close, I pulled away until it became too painful for my scalp, then abruptly head butted him. Oh, my! I finally had something to put on my to do list. I was going to need to be checked for a concussion. I made contact dead center with his face.

Other than him rubbing his nose, he showed no sign of pain before he licked my cheek. "I knew you'd be amusing."

Suddenly, Sticks bounded through the brush, tackling Mac from the side and taking both of us down with him. Both men easily recovered, somersaulting away from one another then standing with their fists in front of them, ready to do battle, neither of them breaking eye contact with the other. I, on the other hand, stayed down, moving behind a tree for protection.

"Why don't you just give up, Torres? You're the one with a weakness. That little lady is in your head.

You're wondering what I am going to do to her if you fail."

Sticks once again came at Mac. This time Mac moved out of the way, but not before clipping Sticks's jaw. "Keep coming at me, Torres. You've gotten soft while being a top agent, sitting at a desk, telling others what to do." They circled each other some more. "You're getting tired. It's only a matter of time. I only have to wait you out."

They had similar muscle mass, but Mac had a few inches in height over Sticks. Mac looked more formidable in his black t-shirt with beige cargo shorts, whereas Sticks's Hawaiian shirt took the "fear me" factor down a notch. But I had faith in my former pretend husband.

Foregoing his words to wait it out, Mac lunged at Sticks, who turned at the last minute, jumped, twisting in the air, and landed a kick to Mac's chest. Sticks had a trickle of blood from his lip and Mac was slightly bent but still in a defensive stance. Sticks lowered his center of gravity as well, not wanting Mac to be able to rush him again. It reminded me of wildebeest bucks on National Geographic documentaries lowering their heads before ramming each other.

Sticks was the first to move. He dove at Mac and both men gave and received blows to the stomach. The flaps of Sticks's shirt hid most of the action, but I could tell from the sound that the punches were hitting their mark. At one point, Sticks swept out with his foot, landing a kick below Mac's knee. Mac regained his balance, put all his weight on his other leg, then resumed the fight.

A plane flew overhead. Mac stopped then pulled out a gun and aimed it at Sticks. "I was going to take you down myself, hand to hand combat. Prove that you aren't the best, but it looks like I'm running out of time."

Sticks's face was blank. He was so still, I wasn't sure he was breathing. My breathing, on the contrary, had become rapid and shallow. I had never been this frightened. It wasn't because of the gun either. It was how Sticks looked. This could not be the same man I had made love to only hours before. This man was emotionless, empty.

I hunched to the ground, getting lower so there was less of me for Mac to use as target practice, but still on my feet so I could run if needed.

Mac laughed. "You always were good at the silent treatment. You forget I trained right alongside you. I know the same tricks." He stood just as still as Sticks but eventually broke the silence. "I want you to put up a fight. Let me take pleasure in the fact that you think you might have hope."

The men were back to being in a stalemate. I stood and walked onto the path, knife held in front of me. My plan was this distraction would prompt Sticks into action. "I have hope."

It did. Sticks went at Mac low, grabbing his arm while pushing it up and twisted his wrist down. It loosened Mac's grip on the gun and it fell to the ground.

I quickly picked up the gun, aiming it at Mac. It

was similar to Sticks's gun and I was thankful I had made good on my promise to go to the shooting range more often.

As I had been recuperating at home, I told Rad I would give him a discount on his rent if he would teach me how to shoot a Glock. Now knowing what to do, I pulled back the slide and heard the bullet chamber. I had the rear sights lined up with the front sight and was certain there was no way I could miss. Just in case, I yelled, "Sticks, move away from him. I can take it from here."

I bluffed, "What did you teach me, Torres? Two to the chest, one to the head?"

Sticks replied, "You don't need to shoot, Lainee."

Mac moved toward me, one of his arms cradling the other. I started to step away, but it messed up my aim, which was probably his intention. I fired off a shot that missed completely.

Mac kept coming, wincing as he put weight on the leg Sticks had kicked. "Didn't think you could do it."

With the lies I told before, I didn't see a need to return to the virtue of honesty, so I said, "That was a warning shot. Do not come any closer." I raised the gun and double braced my aim, remembering not to cover the back of the slide with my thumbs, and shot again. This bullet grazed his side.

Mac paused, moving one hand to cover his wound. "Closer, but still no prize."

"I think the saying is *close but no cigar*. And here's another one for you, *third time's the charm*."

This stopped him in his tracks. He raised both

hands in the air.

I looked over at Sticks. "No one stands a chance against me."

"You're right, hon. And I think you could have done it without the help."

"Help?" I questioned. "Did Mac hit you too hard?"

I heard a slight rustling behind me.

"Miss Delaney, is it? Put the gun down. I'm First Sergeant Gellar. I spoke with you on the phone earlier. There is another man with me, Sergeant Rockwall. We are part of the team called in at the request of Agent Torres." The man kept speaking calmly. "For our safety, ma'am, we need to make sure you are unarmed before we approach Agent McElhaney."

He was speaking to my back. I didn't want to turn to see if he was telling the truth. The gun was my protection, I wasn't sure I wanted to give it up. However, Mac was the one surrendering and Sticks seemed to trust these new men, so I slowly lowered the gun to the ground.

The men rushed around me to subdue Mac. Sticks and a third man, who had come from the opposite direction, approached me.

"You were great, Lainee," Sticks said.

"I know. I'm still on a high. And not just from me capturing Mac, either."

"But ma'am, Agent Torres dislocated McElhaney's patella and his arm…" Sticks waived off the rest of the man's comments.

I continued, "You should have seen me

navigating the terrain, Sticks. I was marking my path and using survival skills. And the untamed natural wildlife? Handled like a pro." I turned and spoke louder, so all of the men could hear me. "Which reminds me, all of you should be using insect repellant. There are a lot of dangerous creatures on this island."

The third man asked me, "Were you on this island the entire time?" Then turned to Sticks. "Isn't this island less than a hundred acres?"

Sticks put his arm around me. "Why don't we get you to the bungalow? You'll want to lie down once the adrenaline wears off."

"Alright, but," I pointed to the men helping Mac to his feet, "I don't think they are taking my advice about the repellant. You know the mosquito is the biggest threat to humans worldwide."

"These men are used to threats, Lainee. They're well protected." He was patting my shoulder and leading me down the path.

It was then that reality struck. "Oh, my god, Sticks. The Tamblays. I found them. They're dead." My legs were becoming weak. "Oh, my god. He killed them."

Sticks supported me. "Everything's fine, Lainee. You're safe now. Mac isn't going to hurt anyone else."

"He was injured, and he still kept coming at me." Then the biggest realization hit. "And you're just like him. You were trained just like him. You are just as dangerous."

"That's not true."

"You're right, it's not. You're even more dangerous. He said it. You excelled at everything."

"That was simply his jealousy distorting the truth."

"So, there are no top-secret missions you're hiding from me?"

"None at all." He smiled then winced when he hugged me, which was reassuring. Maybe he wasn't the indestructible agent I was imagining.

We made it to the bungalow and Sticks placed me in one of the hammocks. They needed the bed to stabilize Mac's injuries before transporting him.

"Agent Torres, you might want to have someone look at your ribs."

"That's a good idea. Lainee, why don't you rest. You've had an eventful day," Sticks said as he placed a kissed on my cheek then turned toward the man.

I watched as they walked away, expecting to see Sticks submit to medical care, but he never did. He stood upright and walked steadily, directing the other men. Sticks was lying. He was the one in charge.

Chapter Thirty-Nine
Sticks in Stone

I had no idea how long I had been sleeping when a man entered and walked through the living area into the bedroom. He addressed Sticks, "Sir, the boat is here. They're ready for Miss Delaney."

Sticks turned to look at me. I pretended to be asleep. "Let's let her rest some more. I'll tell her when she wakes up."

I wasn't sure I wanted Sticks to tell me anything. Gone was the mysterious agent persona. In that guise, I felt the worst he had done was investigate horrific crimes, possibly being tainted with the evilness of the world, but working to end it. With every person who came in and every phone call he took, that image of him was becoming more and more distorted. Now, I could easily see him as the one who had perpetrated some of those evil acts.

He asked the newcomer. "Do you have any updates?" When the man began speaking, Sticks walked to the bedroom door and closed it.

Trust was gone. This was my chance to get away from him. From everything on this island. I struggled in my grogginess to get out of the hammock, not seeing the young man who had questioned my account of the capture standing at the front door. The inquisitor moved toward me. "Do you need something? I've been instructed to make sure you have everything you need."

"I need to get off the island." I disentangled myself and headed for the pier, grabbing only my handbag with identification documents and, fingers crossed, travel tickets. If not, then there was the hope that I would have enough on my credit card to get home.

"Wait! I have to ask Agent Torres."

"Do what you have to do. I'm not waiting."

I was about to board the boat at the end of the pier when I heard someone yelling my name. It was Sticks. He ran down the ramp to catch up to me. One more sign that he had lied. He wasn't as injured as he had led me to believe.

"Lainee, I almost forgot. I have something for you." He reached into his pocket and pulled out a smooth rock. "I made it after our walk along the beach this morning."

He was being gentlemanly because that was much more than a walk. And this morning had seemed a lifetime ago. "Thanks." I smiled weakly. "A memento from our trip."

"Look at it closer, Lainee."

I turned it over. Rudimentary letters were carved in to the once smooth surface. "It's your name."

"It's carved in stone. To stay. It's not going to wash away with the first wave. I'm not going anywhere."

"Does that mean you aren't going to Arizona?" He had to go. I needed a break from him. I had to determine what was real and what was part of the pretend relationship Sticks and I had built.

"I was referencing more of an emotional level."

Somewhat relieved, I looked at the rock, rolling it back and forth and worrying it with my thumb, then handed it to him. "I'm not sure I'm ready for this yet." *Especially since I think you're lying to me* is what I wanted to add.

He placed it in my hand, leaned in to gently kiss my lips, and whispered, "Lainee, please. Just take it and know I'll be there for you."

I put the stone in my pocket and stepped onto the boat. Once I was seated, Sticks motioned, and the captain pulled away from the pier. Tears formed in my eyes, and with the bile of betrayal rising in my throat, I turned to look at Sticks standing on the pier.

He waved and yelled over the engine, "I'll always be your Sticks in stone, Lainee."

ABOUT THE AUTHOR:

Frances Langley is a small-town girl from Central Texas. Being the youngest of eight children taught her the most important lesson in life: you have to have a sense of humor. She utilizes this humor in her writing.

Frances got the chance to move to the big city when she met her husband while attending Baylor University. They currently live in Fort Worth, Texas, and survive life together while raising three teenagers.

Website:
www.authorlangley.wixsite.com/langley

Facebook:
www.facebook.com/AuthorLangley/

Twitter: **Listen on Youtube:**
@authorlangley   AuthorLangley

Publisher:
www.langleyhousepublis.wixsite.com/publishinglh

Made in the USA
Monee, IL
15 October 2023